No Surrender

J. J. Murhall
Illustrated by Martin Remphry

Hodder
Children's
Books

a division of Hodder Headline Limited

For Saoirse Ruby, Michael and Alfie
(the angel with the dirtiest face).
Ne cedes malis. (Yield not to misfortune.)

Text copyright © 2001 J. J. Murhall
Illustrations copyright © 2001 Martin Remphry

First published in Great Britain in 2001
by Hodder Children's Books

The rights of J. J. Murhall and Martin Remphry to be identified as the
author and illustrator of this work respectively have been asserted by them
in accordance with the Copyright, Designs and Patents Act 1988.

10 9 8 7 6 5 4 3 2 1

A Catalogue record for this book is available from the British Library

ISBN 0 340 81729 1

Printed and bound in Great Britain by
The Guernsey Press Ltd, Guernsey, Channel Islands

Hodder Children's Books
A division of Hodder Headline Limited
338 Euston Road, London NW1 3BH

<u>Case File No. 883</u>

'Rugg! Will you stop staring at that map and come and sit down at once!' Sir Gerald Blenkinsop-Smythe, Director of the Department of Unnecessary Buildings, glared at his colleague from behind his vast desk.

Percival Rugg had arrived in a terrible state, unkempt, babbling on about headstrong children thwarting his every move, eccentric teachers – correction – *highly* eccentric teachers and dinner ladies with malice on their minds.

What he had suggested was nonsense. Ludicrous, even! His assignment had merely been to shut down a school that happened to be in an extremely bad state of disrepair and was being run using methods that were far too relaxed. It was a straightforward enough case. Gather some incriminating evidence and note it down. A novice could have undertaken it.

Sir Gerald sighed heavily as Percival Rugg continued to ignore him and study the map which showed, with various coloured flag pins, all the buildings earmarked for closure throughout the world. There were thousands of them, millions possibly, from Australia to the North Pole (even an igloo wasn't safe, when the D.U.B. came knocking). Percival Rugg, his Chief Inspector and Best Closer Down of Unnecessary Buildings, Regional Gold Medal-winner, 1988, no less, was mesmerized by the blessed thing.

Sir Gerald had seen this particular telltale sign before. He was, after all, an expert in his field, a man with forty years' experience in the successful closure of places. Another inspector had shown exactly these symptoms just a few months previously, having failed to close down the very same building, Rodney Archthimble had also been summoned to the D.U.B. headquarters in London to explain his lack of results.

'Rugg! Didn't you hear what I said? Pull yourself together and take a seat,' snapped Sir Gerald impatiently. 'I need to speak to you about St. Saviour's.'

Percival Rugg yelped and closed his eyes for a moment as he heard those appalling words again – St. Saviour's, St. Misbehaviour's. They haunted his every waking hour. He couldn't sleep, he couldn't eat, he certainly couldn't relax. The school was taking him over, consuming him. Destroying him.

The Inspector began to tremble as he opened his eyes again and scanned the map's surface, his beady gaze darting about as he frantically searched for a particular place. He made a mental note …

Must find its whereabouts. Maybe it will give me some answers. Perhaps a clue on how to rid the world of this despicable, f-f-f-happy school.

Percival Rugg gritted his teeth. He still couldn't conjure up that abominable word without wanting to scream out in frustration.

'What are you actually looking for?' Sir Gerald stood up from his chair and joined his colleague over by the map. He placed a friendly hand on Percival Rugg's shoulder, knowing he couldn't afford to lose him. Inspectors as thorough and meddlesome as Percival Rugg were hard to find these days. The position called for someone who was a major killjoy and

5

all round party pooper. Percival Rugg fitted this bill perfectly. He had few friends, no social life to speak of and lacked any sense of humour whatsoever.

'If you want another assignment I can arrange it,' continued the D.U.B. Director cordially. 'Or how about a break? You're looking peaky, Percival. A change of scenery might do you good. We've a home for orphaned baby elephants in India that urgently needs terminating.'

Percival Rugg sniffed abruptly, composing himself. 'Qing Zang. I'm looking for a place called Qing Zang, Sir Gerald,' he stated. 'If I can just find its location then maybe you could send me there? After I've destroyed – I mean closed down – St. Saviour's, naturally,' he hastily added.

Sir Gerald shook his head gravely. 'But Qing Zang doesn't exist, Percival. I told Archthimble the same thing. It's merely a figment of a child's over-active imagination.' He guided his colleague gently back towards the enormous map. 'You've studied this thoroughly, Rugg, but can you find it?' asked the Director.

Percival Rugg shook his head despondently.

'Of course you can't!' replied Sir Gerald. 'Listen to me. In my long career I've closed down more buildings in cities, towns and back woods throughout the world than any other D.U.B. agent and I have never, *ever* come across that particular place.' He stared resolutely at Percival Rugg. 'Forget about Qing Zang. Forget about St. Saviour's. Go to India and make some baby elephants homeless. I'll send someone else to deal with the school – Darren Jenkins, our latest recruit, perhaps. He's young and keen, just the sort of person we need to go undercover amongst cheeky children.'

Percival Rugg rounded on him, his eyes blazing. 'No one's going to close down that school but me!' he seethed. 'Don't you realize it's nearly destroyed me and now it's my turn to destroy it!'

Sir Gerald stepped back in astonishment as Percival Rugg clenched his fists and began to pummel the wall. 'I've never failed on an assignment yet. I'm the world's best closer down of buildings.' He banged his fists harder, making the map shudder. 'The very best, I say! Buildings and their ultimate destruction are my life's vocation! I love to destroy them! Love it, *love it*, LOVE IT, I say!'

Percival Rugg raced over to the window, dragging his superior along behind him by his tie. 'Look around you, Sir Gerald,' he urged, pointing at the bustling city streets below. 'There are at least eight properties out there within a half-mile radius that I've personally closed down in the past six months: three shops, one hotel, a mini-cab office and a bureau de change.'

Then, before his superior had a chance to reply he hauled him back across the room like a reluctant toddler and pointed to a yellow flag

pinned on the map in the southern half of England. In neat felt-tip pen it clearly said 'St. Saviour's.

'Give me forty-eight hours and I'll give the D.U.B. what it wants, Sir Gerald,' promised Percival Rugg, his expression defiant. 'That eyesore and excuse for a school will be terminated once and for all.' Percival Rugg eyed his boss sternly. 'Have I ever let you down, Sir Gerald?'

Not wanting to antagonize his employee any further, Sir Gerald shook his head. Percival Rugg let go of his boss's tie and nodded briskly. 'Forty-eight hours, Sir, that's all I need.' And with that he turned quickly on his heel and marched out of the office.

Sir Gerald adjusted his tie and stared at the door for a few moments before calmly walking over to his desk, picking up his telephone and dialling a number.

'Hello? Hermitage Home for Sick and Suffering Inspectors? ... Good. Sir Gerald Blenkinsop-Smythe here, D.U.B.,' announced the Director brusquely. 'I shall be sending you another patient within the next few days ... Yes, I'm afraid it's the same symptoms as before ... That's correct. Delusions, paranoia, an unhealthy interest in maps and completely irrational behaviour. It appears to be that school again. Heaven knows why he and Archthimble can't close it down – it's only a *school*, after all.'

Sir Gerald tapped his fountain pen briskly on his desk. 'What's the patient's name? Rugg. Percival Rugg,' replied Sir Gerald firmly. 'And you'd better reserve the special suite for him … Yes, that's right. The one with the bars on all the windows and the comfortable padded walls.' Sir Gerald stared sternly down at the floor, where he noticed that the St. Saviour's flag had fallen and was now lying on the carpet. 'And I think you'd better leave his stay open indefinitely,' he added hastily. 'Because I've a feeling that our Mr Rugg might be with you for quite a while. In fact, a very long while indeed.'

St. Saviour's - 7R
REGISTER

ASH, Kimberley
BARZOTTI, Daniel
BATHGATE, Hogan
BOW, Crystal
BUTLER, Benjamin
CHENEY, Gemma
CLARK, Tyrone
DEADLY
DREW, Phelim
EARLY, Charles
FISHER, Beasley
HEINZ, Chester
HOPE, Avril
LOVEDAY, Ruby
MONROE, Zoe
NICKS, Stamford
PINKS, Mungo
PRICE, Spencer
RODRIGUEZ, Suzette
STEVENS, Bop
SWELLS, Veronica
TOOMEY, Alfie
TOOMEY, Micky
TOPPER, Lee
WEBB, Marcus
WISE, Scarlett

Chapter 1

Lessons in Love

'Look, I've already told you. I'm not coming down until you promise me that Stamford won't try any more funny business.' Mungo Pinks gazed anxiously down at his classmates. Stuck in the middle of the playground, Mungo was perched precariously on top of one of Mr Costello's sculptures. He'd been up there all morning and no amount of coaxing was going to bring him down.

'Listen, Mungo. The whole school knows that what you did was outrageous. Almost siding with the Rugg Rat was a terrible thing to do,' announced Bop Stevens. 'But if M*ss* Bicep's willing to forgive you, then so are we.'

Mungo looked at Bop and the rest of the class sulkily, his left eye twitching agitatedly. 'I appreciate that, Bop. But what about Stamford? He never forgives anyone for anything, especially squealing. Stamford's miffed. He's already hung me upside down out of our classroom window this morning. Everything fell out of my pockets – I've lost my front door keys, and he even nicked my bus fare home.'

The class gazed across the playground and up at the open third-floor window. 'Well at least he didn't let go of you!' remarked Benjy brightly. 'So he can't be *that* cross.'

Mungo looked disgruntled. 'Listen, I'm not taking any chances where Stamford's concerned. I'll stay up here for ever if I have to.' He glanced apprehensively over his shoulder as he clung on to the sculpture. 'He's threatened to do something else to me when he comes back after lunch,' he added nervously. Then he sighed despondently. 'I wish I'd never been fooled by the Rugg Rat, but he promised me all this stuff. I imagined owning all these brilliant things and I suppose it went to my head.'

Benjy nodded sympathetically. He knew what it was like to not have anything of your own. 'But it's like M*sss* Bicep explained,' he replied soberly. 'She said that being greedy is bad and having loads of stuff doesn't necessarily turn you into a better person. In fact, M*sss* Bicep said that it can actually make you quite horrible.'

Mungo sighed. 'Yeah well, I wouldn't have minded 'cos everyone thinks I'm horrible anyway. At least if I'd had loads of stuff I could have been horrible in more expensive trainers than Lee Topper's.'

Bop regarded him earnestly. Everyone knew that Mungo Pinks was a snitch and never to be trusted, but he was beginning to feel a bit sorry for him. Anyone who had Stamford Nicks, St. Misbehaviour's' resident bad boy, after them deserved a little sympathy.

As the bell sounded for the end of lunch the class began to wander away.

'OK then, Mungo,' shrugged Bop. 'If that's how you feel. We'll tell Ms Blank you won't be in for English this afternoon. But you'll have to come down sooner or later because Msss Bicep-Tricep's called an after-school meeting and she's insisting that everyone attends.'

'It must be something to do with the Rugg Rat,' Kimberly Ash said adamantly.

'Yeah, he hasn't been back for days,' added her best friend, Suzette Rodriguez.

'No one's seen him since he told Edwin – now what was it, Suze?' frowned Kimberly.

'That he was going to look for a bulldozer,'

15

Suzette replied.

'Yeah, that's right. I hope he's gone for ever. Good riddance—' said Kimberly.

'To bad rubbish.' Suzette nodded firmly.

Chester Heinz, 7R's brightest pupil, looked thoughtful. 'Perhaps he can't find one. Locating a bulldozer in a city is probably a lot more difficult than it sounds. Who knows when Mr Rugg might surface again? With, or without his mean machine.'

The students of 7R exchanged apprehensive looks. Everyone knew that Percival Rugg was bound to turn up sooner or later. Just like a lingering stain, the phoney *Geography* teacher was proving very hard to shift from the casual clothes of St. Misbehaviour's.

Suddenly, from an open upstairs window, Ms Blank's excited face appeared. 'Hurry up children!' she trilled. 'We've more chapters of my favourite book to get through this afternoon and I also want you to compose a poem entitled "Love – What on Earth Does it Mean?" by the end of the lesson.'

The class groaned and rolled their eyes in exasperation, except for Crystal. Writing a poem like that would take her all of ten seconds. 'Love – What on Earth Does it

Mean?' Well, the answer to that was quite simple. Love means Lee.

She set off determinedly towards the classroom. After the disastrous trip to the countryside a few weeks ago when, once again, Lee Topper had failed to acknowledge her and had even returned her gift (the cheek of him!), she'd decided to change her approach. Crystal Bow may have been a total smitten kitten where Lee was concerned, but she was also one tough cookie, and now it was time for a more radical, ruthless approach.

Up ahead, she could see Lee on the stairs, and without so much as a second glance she swept past him, nose in the air, and into the classroom. Lee frowned, confused. He was getting used to having Crystal Bow hanging off his every word – morning, noon and night. But now there was no sickly smile, no Bambi style eyelashes fluttering back at him. In fact, there was no acknowledgement at all. It was most disconcerting.

Lee shrugged and wandered nonchalantly into the classroom. Strolling past Crystal's desk, he glanced slyly at his Number One Fan. There was still no reaction as Crystal, her pert chin defiantly stuck out, stared straight ahead at the whiteboard. Baffled, Lee took his seat behind her. Being blanked only happened to the likes of Mungo 'no mates' Pinks or that boring swot, Chester Heinz. Lee considered this for a moment before trying a different approach.

'Hey, Crystal. Can I borrow your pen?' he asked coolly, leaning forward across his desk.

Crystal turned slowly around in her chair, gazing at him indifferently. 'No,' came the short sharp reply. Crystal turned and faced the front of the class again. A slight smile flickered across her lips as she sensed Lee scowling at the back of her neck. Her mind was made up.

There'd be no more running around after Year 7's heart-throb. What a wimp she'd been! It was time for Crystal Bow, Super Babe, to take control. By the time she'd finished with Lee Topper, Little Miss Mighty would have him eating out of her hand! Crystal leant back on her chair and languidly tossed her hair.

7R steeled themselves as Ms Blank opened chapter 125 of the deathly dull epic novel, *When Oceans Weep With Love*. However, just as she was about to begin, Mungo suddenly cried out from the playground. Everyone rushed to the windows and saw that Stamford Nicks, his faithful bulldog,

Deadly, and best friend Beasley, had surrounded the stranded boy.

'Help! Help, Miss! Stamford's going to gunk me!' cried Mungo.

Ms Blank opened the window and called sharply, 'Stamford Nicks! What on earth are you doing down there?'

Stamford stared up at her. He was wearing another of his hideous tracksuits (turquoise, silver and cerise), piles of gold jewellery and, Ms Blank noticed with great alarm, he was holding a fire extinguisher. 'Don't worry, Miss. I'll be up in a minute,' he called. 'I've just got a little squirt to take care of first.'

Mungo Pinks clung on to the sculpture as Stamford took aim.

'Right, Mung-Ears, I'm givin' you one last chance. Are you comin' down? Or do I 'ave to blast you?'

Mungo shook his head. 'I'm staying put, Stamford,' he replied adamantly. 'The last time you were this angry with me you stitched me into my anorak. I couldn't get it off for a month.'

Stamford sniggered, remembering his ham-fisted handiwork with a needle and thread.

'Stamford! Show some compassion to your

fellow classmate!' cried Ms Blank. However, her kind words fell on deaf ears and everyone gasped as Stamford Nicks aimed the extinguisher at Mungo Pinks and fired.

In a matter of seconds, Mungo and the sculpture were smothered in a creamy white lather. By the time Stamford had finished and stepped back to admire his work of art, it looked as if someone had stuck a giant meringue in the middle of the playground. Mungo Pinks, his anxious face peeping out from a thick coating of foam, was the cherry on top.

Chapter 2

Walls Have Ears

Mungo finally ventured down from his foamy refuge when M*sss* Bicep-Tricep intervened. 'Honestly, Mungo,' she sighed, handing him a towel. 'You do get yourself into some difficult situations, don't you? I know Stamford shouldn't have done what he did. However, perhaps you'll learn a lesson from this little episode and that's always be loyal to your friends and your school.' The Head Teacher regarded him sternly as Mungo wiped his face shamefully.

'Anyway. We'll say no more about it,' declared M*sss* Bicep-Tricep, heading off towards the school building. 'I've got some exciting news to share with you all, so hopefully that will take your minds off other things.'

Mungo followed her morosely into the hall where everyone had assembled. There was an air of excitement about the place and the whole

21

school was chattering excitedly.

All sorts of rumours were flying around regarding the future of St. Misbehaviour's. There had been talk of a farm being built on the waste ground in front of the school, and of Miss Twine, the Science teacher, coming into some money. Some students were saying that Percival Rugg had disappeared and would never be seen again; others, that he was most definitely on his way back. However, everyone fell silent when M*sss* Bicep-Tricep entered the room.

'Right, children and staff, I've called an urgent meeting this afternoon for three reasons,' the Head Teacher declared, climbing up on to the stage. 'The first is regarding our missing busybody, Mr Glugg. Now I realize that he's been absent for a while now and you're probably all hoping that we've seen the last of him.' A loud cheer resounded around the hall as everyone voiced the same opinion.

M*sss* Bicep-Tricep held up her hand and the noise immediately subsided. 'However, I'm afraid my experience tells me that like the proverbial bad penny he'll come back. His sort always does. You see, Mr Smugg is the type of person who doesn't like to be beaten. Therefore we must be on our guard at all times.'

Bop and Benjy glanced at each other and then out of the window and across the playground. In the fading light they half expected to see the distinctive figure of Percival Rugg striding towards them, frantically scribbling observations into his notebook. However, the playground was empty except for Mr Costello's strange sculptures, including the foam-smothered one.

'Secondly,' M*sss* Bicep-Tricep continued, 'I'd like to bring up the subject of the St. Saviour's farm. Now, 7R will remember their trip to the Little Twitterings nature reserve a few weeks ago and Miss Twine's purchase of a gemstone in the gift shop.'

Seated all together, class 7R turned towards their Science teacher who was sitting bolt upright in her chair, dressed in her spotless white lab coat. Alongside her sat Alberta, her trusty skeleton. The children noted that today the skeleton had a stethoscope slung around her neck instead of her usual knitted scarf. As always, Miss Twine was engrossed in a book – this one was entitled *Mortuaries on my Mind: an Insider's Guide*.

'Well, as it turns out,' continued M*sss*

Bicep-Tricep, 'the gemstone is actually a lot rarer than she first thought. Crystal Bow's parents are jewellers and they have recently valued it at £10,000.'

Everyone gasped and Lee Topper gave Crystal a sidelong glance. Crystal, who was absorbed with filing her nails, stopped and gave him a nonchalant look, before continuing with her manicure. Exasperated, Lee Topper slid down on his seat and shoved his hands in the pockets of his tracksuit bottoms. This was bang out of order! She hadn't even blushed!

M*sss* Bicep-Tricep went on, 'Miss  Twine has kindly donated this money to the farm fund.'

Everyone clapped as Miss Twine looked up suddenly from her book and smiled stiffly back at the pupils.

'Which means we can now expand even further than planned,' beamed M*sss* Bicep-Tricep. 'Therefore, the proposed development of the St. Saviour's City Farm will now have a cow shed and some stables added to it as well as a pig sty, chicken coop and duck pond. Who knows, we might even get Ms Blank to give us some horse-riding lessons?'

Ms Blank looked on delightedly. She longed to own a real live pony of her own. She kept a rocking horse called Daphne in her classroom, but somehow it just wasn't the same.

'Finally, perhaps the most exciting news of all,' continued M*sss* Bicep-Tricep, 'concerns our dear dinner ladies, Philomena and Whitney. I received a phone call this morning from a television company. They've heard all about their unusual recipes and larger than life personalities and have chosen them to front a new cookery programme called *Maths and Margarine*.'

A murmur went up around the hall and

Benjy Butler put up his hand. 'They don't know anything about the ladies' pasts, do they?' he asked, concerned. Benjy was really fond of St. Misbehaviour's' dinner ladies. They always gave him second helpings of everything.

M*sss* Bicep-Tricep shook her head and put a finely-manicured fingernail to her lips. 'That's the school's little secret. Philomena and Whitney are highly respectable dinner ladies now,' she said firmly, surveying her pupils and teachers. 'Their wayward days are well and truly behind them. Anyway, filming starts here first thing tomorrow morning. Naturally, Edwin will be working throughout the night to ensure that the kitchens are spotless and Mr Bateau has promised to be on his very best behaviour. Haven't you, Mr Bateau?'

M*sss* Bicep-Tricep raised an eyebrow questioningly at St. Misbehaviour's' Viking-mad History teacher. He glowered sulkily beneath his helmet from the back of the hall, before reluctantly nodding. Meanwhile, Edwin Fox, the caretaker, waved his feather duster enthusiastically in the air as the children grinned at him.

M*sss* Bicep-Tricep concluded, 'Right, children. I think that's about it for today. Now remember. Keep an eye out for Mr Tugg – I don't think we've seen the last of him. Tell your parents that all donations of carrots, greens and any other animal feed will be gratefully accepted and I'll see you all tomorrow morning for St. Saviour's' television debut.'

As M*sss* Bicep-Tricep retired to her office to check the day's racing results and feed her beloved toads, 7R (along with the rest of the school), ambled out of the building across the playground and on to the street.

'Cor. Fancy the telly coming to St. Mis. We're going to be famous,' declared Beasley Fisher.

Lee Topper, who was walking behind them, stopped and checked his reflection in the wing mirror of a parked car. 'Looking good, Lee, looking good,' he mumbled to himself as Crystal brushed past, ignoring him completely. Lee shrugged and then crossed the road to meet his mates in Year 8, the Glory Crew. He had more important things on his mind than moody girls – like how he could get himself on TV, preferably holding his snooker cue. Lee longed to be famous. That way, the whole world would be able to admire his drop dead gorgeous looks!

*

An hour later the school was deserted, apart from Edwin who, dressed in his usual attire of monogrammed silk dressing-gown, embroidered satin slippers and a pair of rubber gloves, had zealously set to work for a night of thorough scrubbing. He was in his element, alone in an empty school, with nothing but his cleaning equipment and his pet mouse, Wordsworth, to keep him company. Whistling happily, Edwin shoved his head in the oven to give it a really good going over.

A few moments later he emerged, puzzled. Scouring pad in hand, the caretaker stared uneasily around the canteen. He'd had the distinct feeling that someone was watching him. However, the room was empty. Edwin shrugged, stuck his head back in the oven and continued his vital work.

A minute later, a shadowy figure stepped out from the side of the fridge and stood, stock still, watching him intently. 'Hello, Edwin. Still cleaning like a man possessed, I see.'

Alarmed, Edwin jumped, hitting his head on the roof of the oven as he recognized the voice behind him. Brandishing his spray can he stood up and turned around.

'Mr Rugg! What are you doing here at this time of night? You really shouldn't sneak up on people like that. You gave me quite a fright,' he remarked uneasily.

'That was the idea,' answered Percival Rugg snidely. 'The element of surprise never fails.' The Inspector ran his long bony hand along the work surface as he surveyed the caretaker coolly. 'Let's stop playing games, shall we, Edwin? You all know that I'm not a real Geography teacher. Far-fetched sounding places and educating children simply don't interest me.' Percival Rugg picked up an egg whisk and slowly turned its handle. The implement whirred noisily in the silence of the vast canteen. 'But the closing down of buildings does. I heard your Head Teacher's little talk today, by the way. I was hiding in the bike sheds and heard that little blabbermouth Bop Stevens mention the meeting so I listened outside the hall window. I particularly liked M*ss* Bicep-Tricep's comments about me never giving up.' Percival Rugg smirked.

'What do you want?' asked Edwin hesitantly, picking Wordsworth up from the work surface and popping him into the safety of his dressing-gown pocket.

29

'Why don't you leave us alone? The children are happy here.'

Percival Rugg chuckled. 'Happy? Of course they're happy. St. Saviour's is nothing more than a circus, with the teachers as clowns.' He eyed Edwin coldly. 'You lot thought you'd broken me, didn't you? Made me crack up? Well, let me tell you, Mr Fusspot caretaker, old Percy's made of sterner stuff. I almost lost it after the Little Twitterings episode but I've recovered, had a few weeks to collect my thoughts, grown stronger and now I've returned, brighter, meaner and even more determined.'

Edwin gulped, clutching his polish.

'Listen to me carefully, Edwin Fox, you drip in a dressing-gown, because I've come to warn you,' continued Percival Rugg, strolling around the kitchen peering nosily into pots and pans as if he owned the place. 'Tell those children that the school isn't safe any more. They need to be on their guard, just like I've had to be on mine. Because tomorrow, or the next day, or possibly the day after that, when the wretched place is as quiet as a mouse and vulnerable, just like it is now, I'll strike.' He gazed coldly at Wordsworth, who was peeping out of Edwin's top pocket. The rodent's nose twitched frantically and then ducked out of sight. Edwin nodded nervously, but didn't reply.

'Think on, Edwin Fox,' declared Percival Rugg, unscrewing a coffee jar and gingerly sniffing its contents. 'Tell those children not to bother coming to school any more, because basically there won't be one. It'll be nothing but dust and memories for them soon.' And with that he tipped the entire contents of the jar all over the floor before turning on his heel and leaving.

Edwin, alone again, shuddered. He was already imagining the terrible mess there'd be when Percival Rugg razed the school to the ground. It was going to take more than a vacuum cleaner to clear that lot up.

Chapter 3

Lights!

Camera!

Lunch!

Philomena and Whitney had surpassed themselves. They'd turned up for their first TV appearance dressed not in their usual nylon overalls, but in glorious floral ensembles from head to toe. Both were wearing billowing flower-print dresses, with matching snazzy new specs. Whitney also wore a wide-brimmed straw hat, peppered with paper flowers, and Philomena had a single red rose stuck behind her ear. Even though they looked like they were off to a wedding, not about to host a cookery programme, the director, an excitable and enthusiastic character called Simon, was delighted with their appearance.

'Perfect!' he declared, positioning them behind the gleaming kitchen work surfaces as the crew adjusted the lighting. 'You both look a picture. This is a great image for our latest celebrity cooks. Soft on the outside but tough on the inside, I'd say.'

Philomena and Whitney looked very pleased with themselves as Edwin waited anxiously in the wings. He knew he urgently needed to tell the S.O.S.S.S. members about his nocturnal encounter with the Rugg Rat but so far hadn't had the chance. The whole morning had been chaotic since the film crew arrived and had practically taken over the place. Now every pupil was trying to cram into the already overcrowded canteen. Edwin spotted Bop and Benjy in the middle of the heaving throng, but he was unable to catch their attention. He sighed and decided to leave it until afterwards.

'Wot about havin' a kid in the show as well?' asked Stamford Nicks, pushing his way determinedly through the crowds to get in front of the cameras. 'I can cook,' he declared arrogantly. 'In fact, you could do a programme all about me an' Deadly an' call it *A Dog's Dinner*,' he added hopefully.

Beasley, who'd followed him, gazed up at his friend incredulously. 'But you've never cooked anything in your life before, Stamford,' he scoffed. 'Even boiling a kettle is a mystery to you.'

33

Stamford stared at him haughtily. 'Well that's where you're wrong actually, 'cos I cooked me mum an' dad an' bruvvers a four course meal once.' The director looked impressed.

Beasley smirked. 'Oh yeah, I remember,' he replied, nodding thoughtfully. 'That was in your last flat wasn't it? The one that burnt down?'

Disgruntled, Stamford said, 'Listen. How many times 'ave I told you, Beas? That wasn't my fault! How was I to know you couldn't fry chips in a microwave? The thing caught fire after it blew up. It was a tragic accident. It could 'ave happened to anyone.'

The director stared dubiously at the big boy and then at his bulldog. Deadly looked pensive as he remembered that particular occasion, although he couldn't have been more than a pup at the time.

'I'm afraid you'll have to take the dog outside,' Simon said curtly. 'Canines and cookery just don't mix. It's very unhygienic having an animal around food.'

'Oi! I'll have you know there's nuffink unhywotsit about my Deadly,' snapped Stamford, looming menacingly over the director. 'He has a bath more often than me dad!'

The director stepped back hesitantly as Beasley put a hand on Stamford's arm. 'Leave it, Stamford. Cooking's boring, anyway.'

Stamford nodded and picked up a fish slice, flexing it threateningly. 'Yeah, you're right, Beas. All that baking cakes and wearing aprons, it's soppy. I reckon cookin's for wimps.'

Whitney leant towards him and snatched the fish slice out of his hand. 'And what do you mean by that?' she asked, rapping him over the knuckles.

Stamford grinned feebly back at her and held up his hands defensively. 'No offence, Whits,' he replied, hastily. 'There's no way you an' Philomena are soft. Wot I *actually* meant was, cookin' takes skill an' you 'ave to be really clever to do it.' He gulped as the dinner lady surveyed him disapprovingly. You didn't mess with the ladies who cooked lunch! No way! Even someone as tough as Stamford Nicks knew that. After all, he was used to dangerous women. His mum was probably the deadliest female on the planet!

Meanwhile, Benjy Butler stood on tiptoe in the crowd trying to get a better view. He couldn't have cared less about the ladies' shady pasts. He was proud of them. They'd managed to evade capture for months, but eventually had been convicted and sentenced. Then they'd escaped, gone on the run to Spain, been recaptured and finally served out the rest of their sentences in the prison kitchens, doing the washing-up.

All that stuff in the papers about their criminal activities had been grossly exaggerated anyway. 'Costa Del Cook Crooks' the headlines had read. Another had splashed Philomena and Whitney's smiling faces across the front page, demanding, 'Are these the Pastry-faced Poisoners?'

M*sss* Bicep-Tricep had known Philomena and Whitney for years. They'd been at school together. As she was a great believer in always giving people a second chance, the kindly Head Teacher had taken the pair under her wing on their release and given them a job at St. Misbehaviour's. As far as she was concerned the unsavoury case was now well and truly closed. They were making a fresh start. Besides, as the Head Teacher had so rightly pointed out, it had all happened a very long time ago, before the students of 7R

36

had even been born.

'What are you going to cook?' Benjy called out eagerly.

'Something vegetarian, I hope,' said Hogan Bathgate, who was standing beside him. 'A nice nut cutlet or turnip stew. Show the viewers that being a veggie is really cool, man.'

Lee Topper threw him a disdainful look as he pushed past. He thought Hogan's taste in food left a lot to be desired. You'd never catch St. Misbehaviour's' very own eco-worrier setting foot inside a fast-food restaurant. In fact, Lee had seen him only last week protesting outside a burger bar on the High Street. Lee had been so embarrassed, he'd crossed over the road to avoid him.

'Perhaps you'd like to get up there, Hogan? Whip everyone into a frenzy with a delicious meal of crushed birdseed and recycled fish food,' Lee said sarcastically.

Hogan ignored his classmate. It was no use arguing with a boy who thought that saving the planet was just another computer game.

Whitney held up an exercise book with the St Misbehaviour's school logo on the front, a toad (M*sss* Bicep-Tricep's favourite animal) wearing a party hat. Below it were the letters

F.M.F., which stood for the new school motto, 'Freedom Means Fun'.

'Well, as the series is going to be called *Maths and Margarine*, we thought that perhaps there should be a school theme running through the programme,' she declared, smiling at Benjy, her favourite pupil. 'All our recipes for the series are listed in here.'

The exuberant director clapped his hands together delightedly. 'What a brilliant idea. We can have a book to tie in with the series. Why not go one step further and have all the recipes based around lessons? Encouraging kids to eat healthily. It looks like we could have a hit on our hands, guys!' he said, beaming at the camera crew.

With a surgeon's precision, Philomena began to meticulously lay out the kitchen implements as Whitney read from the chosen menu. 'Dish of the day—' she began.

'Lee Topper!' a shrill voice called

out from the back of the hall. Crystal scowled, trying not to let her emotions show. Did every girl in Year 7 have to fancy him as well? 'Get in the queue,' she muttered under her breath. The Ice Maiden was starting to crack – she knew she had to try harder!

'Dish of the day,' repeated Whitney firmly. 'Fraction pasta bake. Followed by an Historical flambée. Finished off with a simple sonnet sorbet.'

'Ugh. Sounds 'orrible,' said Stamford, whose diet consisted of chips, chips and more chips, plus the occasional pizza, preferably covered in chips.

'Right. If we could have some silence please,' announced Simon, as the make-up girls fussed over Philomena and Whitney for the final time. 'Now, I want you ladies to behave normally as if you're preparing an average school dinner. Just explain to the cameras what you're doing step by step,' said Simon. 'Now, are you ready, girls?'

'We certainly are, darlin',' chuckled Whitney, smoothing down the front of her dress and polishing her specs with a napkin.

'Ready as we'll ever be,' added Philomena, checking her lipstick in a saucepan lid.

'Right, then. Lights, camera, action!' shouted Simon, and as he stepped back the cameras began to roll.

A moment later the director stomped on to the set. 'Cut! Cut! Cut!' he shouted as Lee Topper's dashing figure strolled in front of the cameras and posed nonchalantly against the counter, chewing gum. Lee stared moodily into the lens, copying his favourite film star.

'Move out of the way!' demanded the director.
'Why?' Lee shrugged. 'I'm so handsome I

should definitely have my own show. Strictly no guests, just me talking all about myself and how great I am.'

'Look. No one's getting their own show except for the dinner ladies,' snapped the director irritably. 'But if we do decide to make a cookery programme for kids then you'll be the first to know.' Lee Topper stared at the floor sulkily before reluctantly leaving the set to rejoin the audience. 'I'm sure your dinner ladies are getting very hot under these lights, so can we begin again, please.'

The pair nodded as Philomena mopped her brow with a dishcloth. Finally the cameras rolled again and the two dinner ladies, in a flurry of floral frocks and fish slices, began to cook. They were naturals in front of the camera. It was as if they'd been born to perform. They laughed and joked, they even sang a duet together and by the end of filming had exhausted the effervescent Simon with their boundless energy.

A round of applause erupted as anyone who hadn't managed to squeeze into the heaving canteen peered through the windows instead. Whitney and Philomena took a bow, gave each other a high five hand slap and then sat gratefully down to survey their delightful dishes.

The director stepped forward. 'OK, well done everybody. We'll resume again this afternoon to film the dessert.' He put his hands on his hips and surveyed the children. 'Oh and by the way, if there's anyone else in the audience who's contemplating taking over the set, forget it.'

Lee averted his eyes and Stamford sneered. Fame would have to wait for both of them.

At the back of the hall, a shadowy figure lurked behind the curtains and watched as the pupils began to slowly make their way out into the playground. Through the crack, Percival Rugg spied Edwin hurrying towards Bop Stevens, the ghastly child who'd instigated his capture in the woods a few weeks ago.

Percival Rugg grimaced. He was a cocky little devil, that kid. Always showing off during registration, trying to wind him up. He wouldn't be so confident when his beloved school no longer existed. Percival Rugg made a mental note ...

After destruction of St. Saviour's remind yourself never work with children or animals again. Even consider a possible career change. TV, perhaps?

Percival Rugg waited until the coast was clear and then hurried over to the set. He walked in front of one the cameras and leered into the lens. He made another mental note ...

Maybe I could host my own quiz show and call it <u>Whose Building Was That</u>?

Chapter 4

Kids in Charge

'Have you told M*sss* Bicep-Tricep about this?' Bop asked, sounding worried. It was lunchtime and he and the rest of 7R had gathered in the bike sheds to speak to Edwin.

The caretaker shook his head dispiritedly. 'She had an appointment first thing this morning with her solicitor and now she's driving to Wales to buy a retired pit pony for the farm,' he replied. 'She won't be back until tomorrow. What are we going to do?' he asked anxiously. 'We can't even call her. You know M*sss* Bicep can't abide mobiles. Instruments of the idle, she calls them.'

Bop sighed. 'Trust M*sss* B to disappear at the first sign of a TV camera. She hates the limelight.'

Benjy nodded. 'Yeah. She'd much rather stay in the background and let everyone else take all the glory.'

'But we need to do *something* – and quickly,' urged the caretaker. 'Percival Rugg says he'll attack the school when it's empty.'

Bop thought hard and watched as the Woodwork teacher, Mr Holliday, or 'H' as he was known, strolled across the playground carrying some planks of wood. The kindly teacher looked as if he didn't have a care in the world. Harry Holliday was a very old man and he loathed the modern world outside St. Misbehaviour's' gates. The school was his life.

Bop looked at him anxiously. Where would 'H' go if St. Mis was closed down? Who'd employ a Woodwork teacher well past retirement age, and who was hopeless at building things? Bop bit his lip thoughtfully and then his face brightened as an idea took shape. 'Bop! You're a genius!' he suddenly exclaimed. 'It's simple. We just won't leave the building unattended. We'll stay put and barricade ourselves in.'

Stamford looked dumbfounded. 'Wot? You mean not go home?' he frowned. 'But we'll miss our tea,' he added, sounding put out.

Bop regarded his classmate soberly. 'Look Stamford, our school's safety is at stake and we've got to fight for it. You know, sometimes you have to make sacrifices, and that even includes missing a meal occasionally.'

Hogan nodded enthusiastically. 'Yeah, Bop's right, man. We're not going to let some pen-pushing dictator walk all over us. War is a dirty business and I'm a peace-loving boy, but hey, there comes a time in every kid's life when he or she must stand up and be counted.'

Chester looked horrified. 'War! What do you mean, war? I can't abide violence,' gasped the school's brainiest, and most passive, boy.

'Listen. I'd rather call it a peaceful protest,' Bop said calmly, as the whole class began to talk excitedly about going into battle against the phoney Geography teacher. 'If the school's occupied then obviously the Rugg Rat can't demolish it. We've just got to guard it, until M*sss* B gets back. She'll know what to do.'

The students of 7R exchanged delighted looks.

'Suits me,' Benjy announced brightly. He hated going home and the chance to move into St. Mis permanently sounded brilliant.

'But what do we tell our parents?' asked Chester, still not convinced. 'My mother and father might always be

46

preoccupied with their work, but I think even they'd notice if I didn't come home for a few weeks.'

'That's simple. We'll tell them M*sss* Bicep's organized a mass sponsored sleepover to raise funds for the school's farm,' said Bop, thinking fast now. 'Besides, I don't think the Rugg Rat will wait much longer. M*sss* Bicep says that the D.U.B. normally likes to have a building shut down and boarded up within a fortnight and the Rugg Rat's been sniffing around this school for nearly a whole term now, so he's well overdue. Time's definitely running out for him– that explains why he confronted Edwin. I reckon he's trying to scare us off the premises.'

Bop looked at his classmates determinedly. 'It's just a hunch, but I think he'll strike early, possibly tomorrow morning. So all we've got to do is stay put, dig our heels in and be ready for him, when he comes. I'm not taking any chances where the Rugg Rat is concerned. I'm ringing my parents right now to tell them I won't be home tonight. We need as many of us to stay as possible. This needs to be undertaken like a military operation. Guards on the gates and patrolling the playground. Lookouts positioned up on the roof as well.'

Hogan stuck his hand in the air. 'I'll go up there,' he said eagerly. 'I'm used to climbing things. I've been up on the school roof before to rescue a stranded pigeon. It's brilliant, you can see for miles. I'll be able to tell you if the Rugg Rat's coming, even if he's still in the next city.'

Bop nodded. 'That's great, Hogan. Perhaps Chester could make a rota for everyone involved. Who's on night watch, playground duty, stuff like that.'

Chester nodded enthusiastically. He was an expert at compiling lists.

Benjy's eyes shone with excitement. In the few short months that he'd been there, St. Misbehaviour's had looked after him, and now it was his turn to protect it.

'Once the TV crew have gone for the day,' Bop continued, 'we lock the gates and then no one gets in or leaves, unless they say the password which obviously every pupil knows.' Bop smiled as his classmates exchanged knowing looks. It began with 'Q' and ended with 'g', naturally.

'OK, that's settled then,' Bop announced. 'We'll synchronize watches and inform the others.'

Just as Bop checked his watch, Simon emerged from an enormous trailer which was parked in the playground, and walked back towards the canteen with the others. 'Whitney and Philomena have been swapping recipes with me,' he smiled. They tried to appear enthusiastic but somehow, the filming of *Maths and Margarine* didn't seem quite so exciting any more. Not when they were about to try and save their school from a spoilsport.

Once again, when the coast was clear, a familiar figure crept out from behind the trailer. Carefully, Percival Rugg tiptoed across the playground towards the school gates, quickly crouching down behind a sculpture as a pupil, late back from lunch, passed close by. Percival Rugg then made a dash across the playground, ducked down beside the wall of the bike shed and saw the stars of the show, the deadly dinner ladies hurrying towards the canteen. He made a mental note ...

Before picking up the bulldozer, dig up some info on that pesky pair of pie poisoners.

Percival Rugg shuddered as he remembered his terrible ordeal when he'd sampled their infamous Din Din Special. He added another mental note ...

Do they have bottles of poison? Possibly hidden in the spice rack?

Chapter 5

One Boy and

His Broom

The rest of the day's filming went without a hitch. There were no more interruptions, as the pupils of St. Misbehaviour's now had far more pressing things on their minds than simply smiling for the cameras.

Word of the impending siege had spread like wildfire around the school. Edwin was given the task of informing the teachers. Calls had quickly been made to parents explaining about the sudden change of plan at home time. Every mum or dad bought the sponsored sleepover explanation and even Stamford Nicks' parents had agreed to let their son off burglary duty for the night, although they did draw the line when it came to sponsoring him. 'We only *take* money, Stamford. We never *give* any away,' his mum had declared when he'd called her.

A while later Bop and Benjy were waving the camera crew's truck off for the day. 'See you tomorrow,' called Simon, leaning out of the window as the lorry sped away.

'Hopefully, if the place is still here,' mumbled Benjy, as he and Bop closed the school gates firmly behind them. Benjy stared across the playground where the pupils were already preparing themselves for the blockade. Luckily, the dinner ladies always bought in bulk and enormous sacks of flour were now being dragged from the kitchen and piled up

against the windows along with bags of sugar, rice and anything else obtained from the ample larders. Empty milk crates and tea chests were also being utilized as makeshift barricades. All around them, teachers and pupils alike were working together.

'Who'd have thought that all those weeks ago, when we first found the Rugg Rat's note lying in playground, we'd end up having to do this,' Benjy declared.

'The school's worth fighting for,' Bop replied, watching as Philomena and Whitney, determinedly set about carrying supplies from

the store room to the canteen. The ladies waved across at the two boys. 'We need to make sure we're well stocked up,' Philomena called out. 'It's going to be a long night and we've Mr Bateau to feed as well.'

'Fame obviously hasn't gone to their heads,' grinned Bop. He watched as the gluttonous History teacher blustered about, barking out instructions to a group of students in Year 8 who were standing around in a circle staring vacantly at some scraps of wood.

'Great slathering hounds of war,' bellowed Mr Bateau, striding towards Bop and Benjy. 'I've just suggested that 8B build a Trojan horse, but the little peasants are just looking at me as blankly as a Saxon's mind.'

Bop glanced at his friend. 'Um, what's a Trojan horse, Sir?' he asked apprehensively. He wished Chester was nearby. He'd definitely know the answer.

'Great Nordic nose pickers, Bop! Don't tell me *you* don't know what it is either?' snorted Mr Bateau. 'Honestly, my History lessons are wasted on you lot. I'm seriously thinking of retiring and setting sail on my Viking house boat after all this is over.'

Mr Bateau surveyed the boys

from beneath the rim of his helmet. 'A Trojan horse was a wooden structure that the Greeks hid in so they could attack a place called Troy without being detected,' he explained brusquely. 'Great Nordic head bangers, I simply thought that if we built one, we could hide in it and then jump out and put some good old Viking wind up Mr Rugg when he turns up.'

Bop and Benjy glanced dubiously at their History teacher. 'Err, that's a really good idea, Sir,' said Bop, uncertainly. 'But wouldn't it take ages to build? It must have been enormous and we haven't got much time. In fact, we've probably only got a matter of hours before Mr Rugg returns. Maybe you could think about building something a little less ambitious instead,' suggested Bop, smiling hopefully at his History teacher. 'A rocking horse perhaps? Like Ms Blank's?'

'Yeah, and maybe we could build a Trojan thingy next term, as part of a "Live Like a Greek Who's Been Stuffed Inside a Horse" project. It could be really huge. Big enough to take the whole school, including Stamford,' added Benjy encouragingly.

Mr Bateau pondered for a moment scratching his beard thoughtfully. Then he perked up. 'Great Nordic toe crushers, Benjy. That's a splendid idea. I'll go and speak to that ancient peasant man Harry Holliday about it right away.' And with that he stomped off in search of the Woodwork teacher.

'Nice one, Benj,' said Bop. 'At least that should keep him occupied and out of trouble for a while.'

Next they turned their attention to the rest of the teachers. Only two were missing: Idle Nigel, the apathetic PE teacher who'd gone to sort out the sleeping arrangements, naturally; and Mr Costello. No one was concerned about the Art teacher's whereabouts because Mr Costello was undoubtedly the world's most anti-social and angst-ridden artist; he was always disappearing. Sometimes he'd go missing for days, but eventually he'd surface again having spent the night beneath some canvases or hidden within the depths of his paint-filled store cupboard. He'd be snivelling into his paint-stained handkerchief in complete and utter turmoil over one of his creations.

Crystal Bow, however, had no intention of getting her hands dirty. Instead she'd spent twenty minutes on her mobile to her mum, instructing her to bring a long list of essential items to the school, immediately. These included a sleeping bag, electric toothbrush, her oldest and most treasured teddy bear, pyjamas (strictly her trendiest), a few copies of *Top Babe* magazine, her mini TV set, some light snacks (chocolates, popcorn, those little cheesy biscuit thingies), and a couple of changes of clothes.

By the time she'd finished packing an enormous suitcase for her precious daughter Mrs Bow's head was spinning. 'Honestly, Crystal, darling,' she declared when she turned up at the school gates a while later, laden down with Crystal's top-of-the-range sleepover paraphernalia, 'you didn't take this much luggage with you when we went on holiday to Florida last year.'

Crystal took the case and barred her mum's way as she tried to pass through the gates.

'Can't I come in?' frowned Mrs Bow. 'I'd like to say hello to M*sss* Bicep-Tricep, I haven't seen her in ages.'

Crystal shook her head adamantly. 'Sorry, no grown-ups beyond this point today, I'm afraid, Mum. Besides, M*sss* Bicep isn't here,' she remarked, opening up the case to see if her mum had forgotten anything.

'So who'll be looking after you this evening then?' Mrs Bow asked with concern.

'Oh there are quite a few teachers staying behind. Miss Twine, Ms Blank, Mr Keen – most of them, in fact. Oh Mum, you've only gone and packed the wrong coloured socks,' moaned Crystal. 'They won't go with this top at all.' She sighed, and then remembering that it was actually a *siege* she was supposed to be taking part in, not a fashion show, hastily pulled herself together. 'Still, never mind, can't be helped,' she announced, hustling her mum towards her car. 'Forget about the socks and don't worry about me, Mum, I'll be fine. I'll see you tomorrow after school,' she said, opening the door and practically shoving her mother inside.

'But I thought you wanted me to sponsor you?' said Mrs Bow huffily.

Crystal frowned. 'Oh, the sleepover!' she declared, suddenly remembering. She slammed the car door shut. 'Fifty pounds an hour. That should be enough. Thanks!' she mouthed through the window. And with that she waved her mum off and walked swiftly back to the school gates.

'Halt! Who goes there?' announced Beasley Fisher, who was now standing guard on the other side of the gates, with Stamford.

Crystal gazed at them coolly. 'Its me,' she announced.

'Who's me?' asked Stamford.

'Me! Crystal! Now stop playing childish games and let me in,' she snapped impatiently.

Stamford peered at her through the railings. 'Well, it looks like you. But how do we know that you're not in disguise? You might be Percival Rugg dressed up as a girly.'

Beasley sniggered as Crystal put down her case and stamped her foot. 'Oh don't be so ridiculous!' she exclaimed. 'I'm Crystal Bow. I'm twelve years old. I live at 5 The Grange and I'm getting very, *very* angry. Now kindly unlock these gates before I do something I just might regret.' Crystal was still a little annoyed at having been brought the wrong coloured socks and she didn't take too kindly to being messed about.

'All right, all right – keep yer bunches on,' replied Stamford, hastily unlocking the gates and letting her in. 'It was only a joke. Cor, some girls 'ave got no sense of humour wotsoever.'

Crystal threw him an angry look as she passed by. 'The only joke around here is you, Stamford Nicks!' she announced sharply.

Beasley nudged his friend as Crystal flounced across the playground. 'I think she's got a soft spot for you,' he said, winking at his mate.

Stamford gave him a smarmy look. 'I'm not surprised. It must be my charmin' personality and stunnin' good looks wot does it.'

'Yeah, must be,' replied Beasley, turning away as he stifled a laugh.

'Halt! Who goes there?' Stamford suddenly announced, as two more figures approached the gates.

'It's us, Stammie. Your mum and dad,' said Mrs Nicks. 'We were in the area and thought we'd see how you and Deadly were gettin' on.'

Mrs Nicks' face abruptly went ashen as she stared down in horror at the padlocked gates. 'Stamford, you're locked in!' she gasped, putting a chubby hand to her mouth in alarm.

Stamford nodded.

'But this is terrible, Wilf,' Mrs Nicks cried in trepidation to her husband. 'Our boy's been imprisoned in his own school!' She stared imploringly back at

Stamford. 'I never thought I'd see you behind bars quite so soon, Stamford,' she wailed.

'It's all right, Mum,' Stamford said hastily. 'It's all legit. I really don't mind. In fact I wanna be here.'

This declaration only made his mum wail louder. 'Did you hear that, Wilfred? Our little Stammie actually *wants* to be locked up! This is terrible. I can't believe it. You're a juvenile delinquent, Stamford! On the brink of becoming an out and out villain! You're not *supposed* to enjoy being behind bars.'

Mr Nicks shook his head despairingly at Stamford. 'You've let me down, son, and now you've upset your muvver. Open these gates immediately and escape like a true Nicks would,' he ordered gruffly.

'Free yourself, Stamford,' his mum beseeched as she gripped the railings. 'Make a run for it while you still can!'

Stamford shrugged. 'I can't, I haven't got a key,' he lied.

Mrs Nicks looked even more perturbed. 'Quick! Give me them bolt-cutters,' she said, snapping her fingers impatiently at her husband.

Mr Nicks looked sheepish. 'I've forgotten

them, Rita. I only bought the blow torch and glass-cutter along tonight. I didn't think we'd be needing bolt-cutters,' he shamefully replied.

Mrs Nicks scowled. 'You mean our son's a jailbird and we can't even get him out? Call yourself a criminal? You should be ashamed. We'll have to go back home an' get them.' She turned back towards Stamford and slapped his cheek tenderly through the railings. 'Don't you worry, Stammie, Mummy will save you. Stay where you are and me and yer dad will be back later. Keep yer chin up and we'll have you out quicker than you can say, "Hold it right there, Nicks. You're nicked".'

Stamford and Beasley watched as Mrs Nicks continued to nag her husband about his forgetfulness as they set off back up the road.

'That's all we need,' said Beasley. 'Over-protective parents getting in our way.'

Stamford glanced moodily at his friend. 'Look, it's not my fault if me mum an' dad care about me. They've always fussed over me, ever since I was a little kid an' they stole me my very first gold chain.'

Stamford brightened up as he saw a familiar figure scurrying across the playground towards the canteen. Mungo Pinks was carrying some sacks, eager to make amends for almost snitching on the school.

'Oi, Mung-Ears. Over 'ere,' called Stamford. He grinned at Beasley as Mungo put the sacks down and hurried towards them.

'I've decided we're goin' off duty, Beas,' said Stamford. 'Mungo can stand guard for a while and when me mum an' dad get back we'll let him deal with 'em. See if he can stop my mum, or Percival Rugg for that matter from gettin' in.'

Beasley chuckled as Mungo approached tentatively. 'What's up, Stamford?' he asked nervously. 'You're not going to try anything funny, are you?'

'Nah! Don't worry. I haven't got a fire extinguisher hidden up me sleeve or nothin'. Besides, I reckon you've been punished enough,' Stamford announced, putting an arm around Mungo's scrawny shoulders. Mungo stared up at him apprehensively. 'Me an' Beasley thought it was about time you 'ad a bit of responsibility, Mung-Ears. So we're putting you in charge of guarding the gates.'

Mungo's face brightened. All afternoon he'd been assigned boring jobs, like fetching and carrying, and taking Ms Blank's rocking horse for a drag around the playground – nothing as exciting as being a security guard!

'Really? Do I get a uniform?' he asked eagerly.

Stamford thought for a moment and then nodded slowly. 'As a matter of fact you do,' he replied. 'Hold Deadly for a minute, Beas,' he said, handing the dog's lead to a bemused Beasley. 'I won't be a moment.' He set off towards the school building, returning a few minutes later, holding an enormous coat and an equally large peaked cap.

''Ere we are, Mungo. Put these on,' said Stamford, holding out the heavy duty overcoat and handing him the cap.

'It looks a bit itchy,' grumbled Mungo, gingerly trying it on for size. The two boys sniggered as Mungo did up the big brass buttons and then put on the hat. He looked ridiculous: completely swamped, lost for ever in the depths of an overcoat. The hem dragged on the ground, the sleeves hung over his hands and the hat's peak stuck out twice as far as his nose and completely covered his eyes.

'Mungo, are you in there?' Stamford laughed. He turned to a giggling Beasley.

'Send out a search party, Beas. Mungo's gone missin',' he chuckled.

'I think it might be a bit too big, Stamford,' Mungo mumbled.

'Rubbish. It looks great, really intimidatin', just like a soldier,' insisted Stamford, guiding Mungo towards the gates. 'Now. All you've got to do is march up and down an' if anyone approaches ask to see their particulars.'

'What are particulars?' Mungo mumbled as Stamford positioned him by the gates. 'Passports, probation forms, video store card, anythin' wot's got a name on it, really,' said Stamford.

Mungo nodded solemnly and then began to march up and down.

Meanwhile, Stamford nipped off again and

returned a moment later holding a broom. 'There's one other thing, Mungo. This is for protection,' he announced, thrusting it at him.

Mungo took it, looking worried. 'Protection? Protection from what exactly?' he asked, still marching up and down. Suddenly he stopped, brandishing the broom like a rifle. 'Do you mean the Rugg Rat?' he whispered nervously.

'Nah! Me mum, actually,' laughed Stamford as he, Beasley and Deadly began to walk away. Beasley was in hysterics as he glanced over his shoulder at Mungo, who now had the broom resting against his shoulder. 'Where did you get that costume from?' he asked gleefully.

'I nicked – I mean I *borrowed* – it from the Drama department,' said Stamford. 'I think it was left over from that soppy show they did last term. Good, innit? It was either that or a sailor suit. I 'ad trouble deciding wot looked more stupid.'

'Where are you going? Don't leave me,' Mungo called despondently at the retreating figures of Stamford and Beasley.

'Keep on marchin', Mungo,' called Stamford. 'Don't stop, mate. Your school needs yer. St. Mis will be relying on yer bravery to stop the enemy from comin' in.'

'What? With a broom?' whimpered Mungo as the two boys and Deadly disappeared inside the school. Mungo looked around him helplessly. It had suddenly got very dark and the playground was eerily empty now that all the pupils and staff had gone inside.

'You got to be brave, Mungo,' he snivelled to himself. 'If you can do this, you won't need loads of stuff to be popular, everyone will want to be your friend.' Mungo imagined being carried triumphantly aloft across the playground by 7R when he stopped Percival Rugg in his tracks.

Mungo Pinks wiped his nose determinedly on his sleeve, adjusted his hat and hoisted up the hem of his overcoat. Then with a steely determination he began to march up and down, up and down, deep into the long, cold night.

Chapter 6
Digging For Dirt

'Oh it's a lovely day.
The D.U.B. is heading your way.
With a spring in his step,
He's ready to wreck—
So you'd better get out of his way!'

Percival Rugg was in fine form. He still hadn't eaten, or slept, or managed to change his clothes, but he'd been singing at the top of his voice all morning.

As he left his flat and hurried up the road, his neighbour, Mr Bagshott, watched him from the safety of his window. Since their last encounter (during which he'd been so roughly manhandled) he'd avoided Percival Rugg, but he noted now that Percival Rugg somehow had a more amiable look about him than usual. The Inspector waved congenially up at him and also to passers by. He even smiled at a toddler in a pushchair and although the child promptly burst into tears it did nothing to impair his buoyant mood.

As he crossed over the road, continuing to hum to himself, Percival Rugg made a mental note ...

You have a fine voice, Percival. Book yourself some professional singing lessons. Who knows? You could become the world's first singing D.U.B. Inspector.

Percival Rugg rounded the corner and approached a building site. His eyes shone with excitement as he saw the gleaming shape of a bulldozer up ahead, its metal cabin glinting enticingly in the early morning sunshine. 'My baby!' he muttered longingly under his breath.

He walked on to the site, stepping gingerly across the piles of earth and past the partially-built houses. He made a mental note ...

When will these properties be completed? Find out and then proceed to close them down.

Percival Rugg approached a Portakabin

and knocked briskly on the door.

'Enter,' a voice called from inside.

The Inspector opened the door and stepped inside to find a ruddy-faced man sitting in a chair with his feet up on a desk.

'Percival Rugg,' declared the Inspector shaking the foreman's hand enthusiastically. 'I called you yesterday regarding the hire of a bulldozer?'

The foreman nodded. 'How long do you need it for?'

Percival Rugg smirked. 'A few hours, no more than that. I think today's going to run very smoothly for me.' He stared meaningfully at the foreman. 'You seem like a man of the world Mr, err—'

'Reed. Jack Reed,' the man replied briskly.

'Mr Reed, or may I call you Jack, perhaps?' leered Percival Rugg, giving him a sickly smile. He was obviously a figure of authority, competent and in control, just like himself. 'I've had a hard time of it lately, Jack,' Percival Rugg continued. 'I was assigned a particularly difficult case. However, I can now see a light at the end of the tunnel.'

The foreman stared back at him incredulously as Percival Rugg eagerly took a seat, his beady eyes shining hungrily with anticipation. 'You see, I've found out some information about certain ladies that will finally blow the lid off a particular place.' He leant across the desk conspiratorially, beckoning for the man to come closer. 'Poison!' he hissed.

'I beg your pardon,' the man frowned uneasily, taking his feet hastily off the desk.

'They were arrested for *poisoning* someone!' said Percival Rugg.

'Who? What? When?' asked the foreman, confused but intrigued.

'Why, the dinner ladies, of course!' announced Percival Rugg triumphantly, his voice shrill with excitement.

The foreman nodded and slowly slid his chair away from the deranged character on the other side of his desk. 'Oh, I see. The dinner ladies,' he said soothingly, as if he were addressing a small child. 'And who did these dinner ladies actually poison?'

Percival Rugg bounced up and down on his chair ecstatically. 'Here's the good part, Jack,' he said breathlessly. 'They poisoned none other than—' He paused and took a deep breath. 'None other than Sir Gerald Blenkinsop-Smythe the First. Sir Gerald Senior!

DEADLY

My boss's father, no less!'

'But why would they do that?' asked the foreman, hardly believing what he was hearing. The man sitting opposite him was clearly nuts.

'They used to cook for him at the D.U.B. headquarters,' continued Percival Rugg fervently. 'And one day they found out that Sir Gerald was going to close down a large and extremely overrun home for destitute women and their children. You know the sort of place,' Percival Rugg sneered distastefully. 'Full of snotty-nosed screaming brats and coarse-sounding women. Anyway, the dinner ladies found out, took offence at this and blatantly tried to poison Sir Gerald!'

'How?' asked the foreman tentatively.

'They tampered with his jam roly poly!' Percival Rugg excitedly declared. 'They could have killed him, save for the fact that Sir Gerald had a meeting to attend and didn't have time to finish it!' Percival Rugg shuddered. 'Goodness knows what would have happened if he'd polished off that dessert. He'd have ended up in that great D.U.B. place in the sky and if he was anything like his son, he'd have probably tried to close *that* down as well if it wasn't up to scratch! Anyway,' continued Percival Rugg, leaning back on his chair. 'He was very ill in the meeting, threw up all over his report, I understand. An investigation was mounted, code named "Operation Sick as a Pig" and those wicked pudding poisoners were eventually charged. And even though the wily women managed to escape and go on the run for a while, they were recaptured and the rest, as they say, is history.' Percival Rugg reached into his pocket. 'Would you care for a wine gum, Jack?' he smiled, offering a very stale packet to the foreman.

Jack Reed shook his head, staring at them fearfully as if they too might be spiked. 'No thanks. Who was it you said that you worked for, by the way?' he frowned.

'Why, the D.U.B. of course,' declared Percival Rugg proudly. 'The Department of Unnecessary Buildings.'

Almost immediately the foreman's expression began to change and he leapt up angrily. 'The D.U.B.!' he yelled. 'Not that low down stinking lousy place?' He pointed out of the window. 'We work hard building homes for people to live in, offices for them to work in, and what do you lot go and do?'

'Close them down,' smirked Percival Rugg, popping a wine gum smugly into his mouth.

'That's right!' blustered the foreman. 'As fast as we build them you come along and shut them down. It's outrageous! There are homeless people on the streets, living in cardboard boxes and you're busy destroying places.'

Percival Rugg stared at him coldly and made a mental note ...

Remember to check out those cardboard-box residences under the viaduct. Close them down forthwith. Make some homeless people homeless.

'There's no room for sentimentality in my job,' remarked the Inspector indifferently. 'Whether it's a hospital for sick puppies or a refuge for unwanted kittens, it makes no odds to us. As far as the D.U.B. is concerned, if it's not making oodles of money or if the inhabitants are having too much f-f-f—' he choked on his wine gum, unable to say *that* word, 'too much of a good time, then the solution is quite simple. We board it up and close it down!'

The foreman shook his head despairingly. 'And I suppose that's why you want to

74

hire the bulldozer?'

Percival Rugg stood up and reached into his jacket pocket. 'That's right. Now will £100 suffice for a few hours' rental?' he said, pulling out his wallet.

'Forget it. I've decided the equipment's not for hire,' the foreman said gruffly, opening the door. 'Now if you'll excuse me, I've work to do.'

Percival Rugg looked at him in alarm. 'What do you mean the equipment's not for hire? How dare you refuse a D.U.B. Inspector, a *Chief* Inspector, I might add, access to a vital piece of equipment?'

'Simple. I've changed my mind. You're not getting your greedy mitts on my bulldozer!' yelled the foreman before slamming the door directly in the Inspector's face.

Percival Rugg stared indignantly at the door and then his expression darkened as it dawned on him that once again his day was about to go horribly wrong. 'NO! NO! NO!' he shouted. 'I won't allow this to happen.' And he stomped across the site, snarling and growling at the astonished labourers.

Percival Rugg approached the bulldozer and pulled open the door. An astonished driver stared down at him from his cabin.

'This vehicle is being seized by the D.U.B. Kindly vacate it immediately.' snapped Percival Rugg.

'The D.U.-what?' asked the bewildered driver. 'Sorry mate. Only authorized personnel are allowed to drive one of these. You need a special licence.'

'Yes. And I'm a special person!' hollered Percival Rugg grabbing the man by his jacket and hoisting him out. The man landed in a heap on the ground as Percival Rugg jumped into the cabin, switched on the engine and rumbled out of the building site.

'Oi! Come back here with my bulldozer!' shouted the foreman, racing out of his hut.

Percival Rugg stuck his head out of the window. 'Nothing will stop me destroying that school now!' he shouted wildly. 'Not you. Not them. Not anybody! You can never keep a good D.U.B. Inspector down. We'll fight them in the High Street. We'll fight them up the lanes. Wherever there's a condemned building, we'll be there, notebooks at the ready. You'll never beat us. Never! Long live the D.U.B., I say!'

And with that Percival Rugg careered up the road, crushing a litter bin and flattening a bus shelter (empty, luckily) with his brand new mean machine.

Chapter 7

We Shall Not Be Moved

'That was the worst night's sleep I've had since I went camping with the cubs,' Lee Topper declared grumpily, folding up his sleeping bag and combing his luxurious hair.

'You were in the cubs? I don't believe it!' Bop said as he climbed out from underneath his duvet.

'Yeah. When I was a little kid, but only for a week, mind,' Lee added hastily. 'All those chores, mowing lawns, washing cars. Too much like hard work, if you ask me. Besides, I didn't like the uniform. It didn't match the colour of my eyes. It was shortly after that that I joined the snooker club,' he remarked happily. 'I was holding my very first cue at the age of six. I had to stand on a box to reach the snooker table, but even then I had a gift for the game.'

Bop smiled at 7R's most arrogant pupil

while Benjy, staring out of the window, suddenly said, 'Talking of uniforms, what's Mungo doing down there on sentry duty dressed like that?' He pointed towards the gates where a tired Mungo was still traipsing up and down. Bop and Lee joined him at the window.

'Oh no. There seems to have been a mix-up,' sighed Bop. 'Chester made up a rota and Suzette and Kimberly were supposed to take over from Stamford and Beasley this morning. Mungo shouldn't even be out there. Not with his track record on loyalty.'

'Wot's for brekkie?' The groggy voice of Stamford Nicks called out from across the other side of the classroom.

Bop, Benjy and Lee turned towards Stamford. He was lying in a foul yellow, brown and mint green coloured sleeping bag. His big face and Deadly's were just visible over the top. Beside him, in two empty jam jars, was his entire jewellery collection. 'I always get me breakfast in bed at 'ome. Me mum brings me chips on toast,' he said, yawning.

'Stamford, why is Mungo guarding our school dressed like an idiot?' scowled Bop. 'You and Beasley were supposed to be out there last night. Not tucked

79

up in bed dreaming about chip butties.'

Beasley slid beneath his duvet as Stamford climbed lazily out of his sleeping bag. Everyone winced when they saw his pyjamas, which were pillar-box red with shocking pink stripes. Stamford looked like a giant stick of rock and, without his jewellery, somehow naked.

'Sorry about that,' shrugged Stamford morosely. 'I meant to tell yer. There was a change of plan.' He opened the window and a chill swept around the classroom. The other boys in 7R huddled beneath their covers. 'Cor, it's a bit nippy out there,' declared Stamford. 'Good job I'm wearing me thermal jimjams.' He stared down at Mungo. 'Oi. Mung-Ears! Did me mum and dad come back last night?' he hollered down to the shivering boy.

Mungo stopped marching and stared back up at him. 'Yes. They were looking for you, but I told them that you'd gone,' he shouted back up. 'They seemed really pleased. Said something like they knew you wouldn't let them down. That a Nicks always manages to escape.' Mungo shrugged. 'I'm not sure what they meant, but they went home happy enough.' He looked at Stamford imploringly. 'Can I come in now? I'm freezing.'

Bop squeezed past Stamford's bulky figure and stuck his head out of the window as well. 'Yeah, sorry about the mix-up, Mungo. We'll send someone down to relieve you soon.'

As Bop shut the window the classroom door flew open almost immediately and the scruffy figure of Hogan Bathgate was standing there.

'I've been on the roof,' said Hogan, blustering in, his unkempt hair looking wilder than ever.

'Care to borrow a hairbrush?' Lee asked drolly.

Hogan ignored his classmate's wry comment. 'I haven't slept all night. All I had was an owl to keep me company,' he said excitedly.

'Terwit! Terwoo!' Lee said sarcastically. 'If it isn't the bird boy of St. Misbehaviour's, no less!'

'Well done for being so vigilant,' said Bop, he too ignoring Lee Topper's rude remarks. 'You and Mungo have put us lot to shame. We spent the night playing cards and listening to Beasley's not-very-scary ghost stories.'

Hogan shrugged. 'I'm used to being vigilant. I have to be in my line of work. Anyway, I've come to tell you that the Rugg Rat's on his way. I spotted him about five minutes ago driving a bulldozer up the High Street, heading in this direction.'

Bop checked his watch. 'Right. Wake the teachers and the rest of the school. We need to get into position.'

'But supposing he breaks down the gates?' asked Benjy anxiously. 'We'll have to evacuate the school.'

Bop shook his head determinedly. 'We'll never abandon the school, Benj. We'll fight him for it if necessary.'

'With wot?' asked Stamford, putting on his jewellery as if it were a suit of armour. 'Even I'd 'ave trouble beatin' up a bulldozer.'

'Well, last night, when you lot were snoring your heads off, I came up with an idea,' said Bop.

Benjy breathed a sigh of relief. Thank goodness for Bop Stevens and his never-ending stream of ideas.

'We'll occupy the kitchens,' said Bop bluntly. 'That way we'll have plenty of ammo to hit him with if he does get through. Philomena and Whitney will give us a hand. Come on. We've no time to lose.' And with that Bop headed off to round up the other pupils and teachers on the floors below.

Fifteen minutes later 7R and 8C were positioned in the kitchen. Whilst outside in the playground, under the command of Mr Bateau and Harry 'H' Holliday the rest of Years 7, 8, and 9 – none of Year 10 were present, they'd all gone on a camping trip – and most of the sixth formers were huddled behind some crates, armed with bags of flour.

'Oh this is fun!' declared Whitney, pulling out another batch of rock-hard rock cakes from the oven. She tested one by throwing it at a light bulb, which promptly shattered into a thousand pieces.

'Perfect!' she announced. 'Hard as nails and twice as deadly.'

Philomena smiled as she chucked some more mashed potato mixture on to a plate and proceeded to fashion them into what she called 'blob bombs'.

'This recipe was handed down to me by my dear old Grandmama,' she pronounced. 'It's a mixture of egg, flour and super glue. Swallow one of them and you won't be able to open your mouth for a week.'

Whitney nodded approvingly as she handed out the cakes. 'I knew we should have administered something a little stronger to Mr Rugg,' she sniffed huffily. 'If you'd have only let us loose on the Din Din

Special on his very first day, then we wouldn't be in this mess now.'

Benjy, who was wearing a saucepan on his head for protection, frowned at her. 'That's enough of that kind of talk, Whits,' he said crossly. 'Do you want to go back to prison? What about your TV career?'

Whitney and Philomena looked ashamed. 'You're right, of course, Benjy darlin',' said Whitney. 'We only poisoned Sir Gerald because he was a cruel and heartless man.'

'And so is the Rugg Rat,' said Benjy. 'But that doesn't mean you can go around poisoning him.'

The dinner ladies sighed resignedly.

'Uh oh! I can hear something coming,' declared Hogan, peering over the sacks of flour stacked up against the window.

'Can you see anything?' asked Bop eagerly. Hogan squinted, as in the distance, on the horizon, he could just make out a speck trundling across the waste ground towards them. 'Stand by everyone,' declared Hogan as the vehicle drew nearer. 'The beast and his bulldozer are on their way.'

Chapter 8

Mungo
The Brave

Mungo Pinks, who was always a little slow on the uptake, didn't see or hear the bulldozer coming until it was looming directly over him like some great metallic dinosaur.

'What the—?' Mungo's mouth fell open as he stared up at the huge monstrosity casting a shadow across the playground. Percival Rugg, seated in the cabin, looked down on him triumphantly.

'Not so brave now, are you, Mungo Pinks?' The evil Inspector glared at him through the windscreen.

'I've never been brave,' gulped Mungo. 'But there's always a first time. You're not coming in, Mr Rugg,' the oily child declared determinedly.

Percival Rugg stuck his head out of the side window. 'Don't be so stupid, boy. Save yourself. Unlock these gates and surrender St. Saviour's to me.'

Mungo shook his head stubbornly. 'I'll never surrender. All my life I've been a liar and a coward. Well, as from today I'm turning over a new leaf. I'll never unlock these gates, Mr Rugg.' He pointed to the paint-daubed sign above them. 'St. Misbehaviour's means something to me. This place is special.'

Percival Rugg shrugged and gazed at Mungo. 'Do you honestly think that a padlock is going to stop me? In case you hadn't noticed, I'm not on a bicycle today. This little beauty can flatten these gates and you in ten seconds flat. Now I'll count to five and if you haven't unlocked them by then, I'll simply drive straight through.'

Mungo gulped again and turned imploringly towards the school.

'Move out of the way, Mungo!' shouted Bop from inside the canteen.

'One!' said Percival Rugg coolly.

'Don't be daft Mung-Ears, do as Bop says,' shouted Stamford.

Mungo didn't move.

'Two,' declared the phoney Geography teacher.

'Great rampaging ruffians, run for it, boy!'

cried Mr Bateau, standing up from behind a wooden crate.

But still Mungo stood his ground.

'Three,' said the Chief Inspector, revving up the engine.

'We'll be friends with you again, Mungo!' pleaded Beasley.

But still Mungo refused to budge.

'Four!' said Percival Rugg callously.

'He's bluffing. He won't really drive through the gates,' said Idle Nigel, who for once was wide awake and raring to go.

'Last chance, Mungo,' shrugged Percival Rugg.

Mungo stuck his chin out defiantly and shook his head.

'Very well then. Five,' said the Inspector.

Everyone closed their eyes as Percival Rugg backed the machine up and revved its engine menacingly. Then he put his foot down on the accelerator and drove the bulldozer straight towards the gates. They buckled a little. Percival Rugg backed up and tried again. This time the gates creaked and bent a little more, however, just like Mungo Pinks they refused to give way.

Inside the bulldozer's cab, Percival Rugg

89

felt powerful, more powerful than ever before, like he was King of the World. Laughing maniacally, the Chief Inspector revved the engine for a final time and drove at the gates with all his might. Finally they gave way and, with a grating sound, toppled over. Percival Rugg drove over the pile of twisted iron and into the playground triumphantly, stopping when he reached the middle. Then he switched off the engine and an eerie silence descended over the school.

'Well, well, well. You have been busy,' announced Percival Rugg. 'A few sacks of flour and a milk crate are certainly going to stop me and my trusty bulldozer, aren't they?' he sniggered.

'Don't come any closer, Mr Rugg. You're already in big trouble for running poor Mungo down,' said Bop, peeping over the sacks, a rock cake at the ready, scanning the playground for any sign of his courageous classmate.

'Ah, Bop Stevens! The troublemaker!' declared Percival Rugg, glaring through his windscreen. 'I thought you'd be behind this little protest. And as for Mungo Pinks, what a stupid child he was. I warned him to move out of the way. And now I'm warning you lot.

Surrender immediately and I'll let you go. Resist, and you'll get the same treatment as the Pinks kid. Now what's it to be? Come out slowly with your hands in the air or take your chances with a ten-ton wrecking machine.'

'No surrender!' shouted Hogan.

'Listen to me. This isn't like the movies, Bathgate,' scoffed Percival Rugg, 'where the hero comes out all guns blazing. This is real life and I've got a bulldozer the size of a small garage pointing straight at you.'

'We don't care,' called Benjy. 'We'd rather stay put than surrender St. Mis to you.'

'Ah, the common voice of scruffy little Benjamin Butler,' Percival Rugg said drolly. 'St. Saviour's' very own answer to Oliver Twist. How's your home life, Butler? Still as appalling as ever, I trust?'

Inside the canteen Bop looked at Benjy sympathetically. 'Don't let him wind you up Benj, that's just what he wants, us losing our tempers, just like he does all the time.'

Benjy nodded resolutely.

'How about you giving the signal to everyone? It'll make you feel a whole lot better,' suggested Bop.

Benjy smiled at his best friend. 'That'd be great. Shall I do it now?'

Bop looked around the canteen. Everyone was in position, including the dinner ladies. 'Yeah, do it now, Benj. Let's let rip on the Rugg Rat once and for all.'

Benjy walked over to the door. He opened it a fraction and poked his face out. 'Oh, Sir. Before you demolish St. Mis can I ask you something?' said Benjy casually.

'If you must,' replied Percival Rugg impatiently. 'But make it snappy. I intend to raze this school to the ground by dusk.'

'Oh, it won't take long,' said Benjy pleasantly. 'Just answer me one thing, Mr Rugg.' He paused. 'Where's QING ZANG!'

Quickly, Benjy put his head back inside as Percival Rugg's expression turned to fury and he let out a blood-curdling scream.

Chapter 9

Food For Thought

Percival Rugg's deafening cry was the signal for the whole school to let rip with blob bombs and eggs. Dozens of them whizzed through the air at an astonishing speed, landing with a resounding splat on to the windscreen. Percival Rugg turned on his wipers in a vain attempt to wipe the mess away. It was hopeless – it went from mash to mush to slush in seconds and as fast as the gunk was removed another batch headed in his direction.

'Stop this at once!' roared Percival Rugg. 'How dare you pelt me with your leftover school dinners!'

Suddenly there was a lull in the onslaught and Percival Rugg peered tentatively through his smeared windscreen. It was short lived, however, as a moment later he reeled back in horror as a mass of what looked like mini meteors came hurtling towards him. Percival Rugg ducked down in his seat as hundreds of the little brown rock cakes made impact with the bulldozer, bouncing off the roof and sides as noisily as giant hailstones on a corrugated tin roof. On and on the attack went as Percival Rugg, his eyes tightly shut, huddled in his cab.

Back in the kitchens, supplies were starting to run low. 'We'll have to resort to using the best china, I'm afraid,' shouted Edwin, fretting about all the mess they were making out in the playground. So a whole artillery of crockery, plates, cups and saucers, even Whitney's favourite pie dish (the Din Din Special one, no less) was commandeered for urgent military use.

Bop opened the door and stuck his head out. 'Do you surrender, Mr Rugg? Or will we have to use more extreme measures?'

Percival Rugg poked his head out through a side window, his expression defiant. 'Pelt me all you like, Stevens. Eventually your kitchens will run dry. And what are your extreme measures anyway? A pancake in the face perhaps?' Percival Rugg sniggered. 'How childish. Just what I've come to expect from such vulgar little savages like yourselves.'

'We're not savages, man,' yelled Hogan Bathgate. 'We're kids, sticking up for our rights!'

A cheer went up from inside the kitchens and from behind the wooden crates in the playground.

'Great shivering Saxons! I'll second that. Let the pesky peasant have it, Bop!' roared Mr Bateau, leaping up again, this time waving a mop ferociously above his head.

'We gave you a chance, Mr Rugg,' said Bop.

'Don't say we didn't warn you.'

'Oh, I'm quaking in my shoes,'  remarked Percival Rugg sarcastically. He sat back in his seat and studied his nails. 'Bring on the dessert,' he said indifferently. 'Although let's hope it's not poisoned as well this time.' He chuckled to himself as Bop slammed the door crossly.

'It's no use. He won't give up,' he said in exasperation. 'Pass us those plates, Whitney. We'll pelt him with some real ammo this time.'

The children of 7R formed a long line from the work surface to the window and items of crockery were handed down it to the pupils in the front line of attack.

'China at the ready,' shouted Benjy, who was holding a particularly large platter. 'Take aim.'

Stamford Nicks, teapot in one hand, sugar bowl in the other, braced himself.

'Fire!' shouted Benjy.

However, the china proved a lot heavier to throw and some of it didn't quite reach far enough across the playground, although Stamford's teapot did hit the target, cracking the bulldozer windscreen right down the middle.

'Bullseye!' Stamford hollered, as Deadly leapt on to the sacks and barked jubilantly through the window.

The Inspector stuck his head out again. 'Sticks and stones may break my bones, but china will never hurt me,' he announced. A lone saucer came spinning towards him and the phoney Geography teacher caught it neatly between his bony fingers like a frisbee. 'What? No cup to go with that?' he smirked, as from inside the kitchen the children realized that they'd finally run out of things to hurl at the Inspector.

97

'We could throw out the food mixer!' said Whitney brightly.

'Or the microwave!' added Philomena, already unplugging it.

Bop shook his head despondently and plonked himself down on a drum of cooking oil. 'It's no use. Nothing's stopping him.' He sighed wearily.

Outside in the playground, Percival Rugg tooted his horn briskly, 'Cooee! Kids!' he called, his voice mocking. 'If you've quite finished with your pathetic attempts at defence, I'd really like to get on with the little matter of destroying your school. Now. One last chance – are you coming out or not?'

Inside the kitchen the children looked at each other resolutely. 'Never! We shall not be moved, man!' yelled Hogan as the sound of the bulldozer's engine began to rev ominously.

'Very well, then. You leave me no choice,' declared Percival Rugg and, putting his foot down on the accelerator, he began to crawl slowly forward. On top of the sacks, Deadly barked ferociously as the menacing machine edged ever closer.

'Is he here yet?' gulped Beasley, pulling his hat further down his head, as if that would somehow save him. Suddenly Deadly, who was being restrained by Stamford, slipped his collar, and squeezing himself through the top of the open window he jumped into the playground, making a beeline for the bulldozer.

'Deadly! Don't be a hero!' cried Stamford, watching as his beloved dog began to attack the massive tyres of the machine.

Percival Rugg opened his cab door and thrust his foot out. 'Get away from me, you notebook-noshing, mobile-munching brute,' he cried, kicking wildly at the bulldog. Deadly abandoned the wheels and grabbed hold of the Inspector's trouser leg instead. He clung on determinedly, swinging around in the air as Percival Rugg frantically shook his leg to free himself.

'Get this beast off me! I can't abide animals,' shouted Percival Rugg distastefully. Deadly's delaying tactics were short-lived however, as a moment later the material ripped and he fell to the ground still grimly holding the bottom half of Percival Rugg's trouser leg between his teeth.

The Inspector quickly pulled his leg back inside the cab and as Deadly stood panting in the playground, 7R peered over the sacks. The bulldozer lunged again, its gleaming grille leering towards them in a wide metallic grin. A strong aroma of petrol wafted into the kitchen and Percival Rugg's maniacal laughter grew louder. 'That dog won't stop me,' cackled the Inspector as the machine finally made impact with the wall, making the whole kitchen shudder.

The children and staff stepped back as Bop jumped up from the drum of cooking oil. 'Yeah, but something else might,' he said determinedly.

'Bop's had an idea!' said Benjy eagerly. 'I knew he wouldn't let us down. What is it?'

Everyone looked at Bop in anticipation as outside, the bulldozer reversed, ready for another attack.

'We're going to surrender. Well at least *pretend* to,' he added hastily, as he watched his classmates' faces drop. 'OK. This is the plan. The Rugg Rat can't stand animals, right?'

Everyone mumbled in agreement.

Bop continued, 'Well then, I think it's time we gave him a really nasty surprise.'

Bop grinned at his friends. 'Toads!' he announced brightly. 'We'll send in the toads.'

The students and staff looked uncertain.

'Look, have I ever let you down yet with the Bop Stevens Guide to Getting Yourself Out of a Sticky Situation?' he asked his apprehensive friends.

Hogan nodded. 'Bop's right, man,' he stated proudly. 'We have to trust him. Just tell us what you want us to do and we'll be right behind you.'

Bop smiled gratefully. 'Well firstly, I want Benjy to go and get M*sss* Bicep's toads from her office,' he announced. 'And then, Hogan, you can sneak out the back way. Let everyone know that I've got a plan and no matter what I say, they're to go along with it, OK?' His friend nodded. 'Be careful though, make sure the Rugg Rat doesn't see you,' he added as Hogan jumped down off the work surface.

'Don't worry, man,' replied Hogan soberly. 'I'm used to hiding from the enemy.' And he headed off towards the back door.

'We also need a large box,' continued Bop. 'A chocolate box would be ideal, something that looks like a present,' he added.

Edwin perked up. 'I've got one that I keep all my poems in,' he announced eagerly. 'I'll go and dig it out from the broom cupboard.'

As the caretaker and Benjy hurried away,

the whole kitchen shook violently as the bulldozer rammed into the wall again, this time shattering a window.

'Right, that's it. I think it's time that me and the Rugg Rat had a little chat,' announced Bop, turning on the cold water tap and splashing his eyes. He turned towards his classmates. 'Do I look as if I've been blubbing?' he sniffed.

Chester nodded. 'Very convincing.'

'Like I'm just about to surrender the school?' stressed Bop, rubbing his eyes vigorously to redden them.

Everyone agreed and Whitney handed him a crisp white handkerchief. 'For added effect,' she said.

Bop took it and shoved it in his jeans pocket, then grabbed a nearby tea towel and strode over to the door. He opened it slightly and waved the tea towel out in front of him.

'We've changed our minds, Mr Rugg. We've decided to surrender,' shouted Bop, poking his head out. Out of the corner of his eye he could see Hogan stealthily making his way around the edge of the playground towards the others, ducking behind a litter bin and using the sculptures to shield himself from prying eyes. From behind the stacked-up crates the pupils and staff stared at each other in disbelief.

'Great stomping wildebeest! What's young Bop playing at?' Mr Bateau frowned.

'Bop Stevens is bluffing. Just you wait and see,' replied Miss Twine with certainty.

Meanwhile Percival Rugg turned off his engine and stuck his head out of the window. 'What's your game, Stevens?' he said suspiciously.

Bop stepped out into the playground. 'That's exactly it, Sir,' he said, walking cautiously towards him. 'We've realized that this isn't a game anymore. It's for real. You're no match for us, Mr Rugg.' He pulled out the hanky and dabbed at his eyes.

'Don't come any closer,' snapped Percival Rugg, surveying him mistrustfully. 'You're up to something. I know you are.'

Bop's shoulders slumped and he sniffed

loudly. 'There's no tricks this time, Sir.' He held his arms out on either side of him. 'We just can't take any more. We've held a meeting and Edwin's decided to surrender the keys to St. Misbehaviour's to you.'

Then, to everyone's amazement, Bop dropped to his knees and began to wail. 'You've won, Mr Rugg!' he bawled, shaking his head mournfully. 'St. Mis is all yours.' Bop let out another loud woeful sob as Percival Rugg stared back at him in astonishment.

He couldn't believe what was happening. The Stevens kid *crying*? Crocodile tears perhaps? He eyed him cautiously, still not convinced. 'And what will your precious Head Teacher have to say about this?' he remarked. 'I know she isn't in school today, by the way. I took the liberty of checking her diary. She certainly won't be very happy when she returns from her little jaunt to find the place shut and her slimy toads out on the street.' He chuckled as he imagined the look on M*sss* Bicep-Tricep's face.

Bop shrugged. 'Just when we needed her most, M*sss* Bicep's gone and let us down.' He sighed and dabbed despondently at his eyes again.

Percival Rugg surveyed Bop smugly. 'Well,

well, well,' he nodded. 'I always had my suspicions that you were a bright boy Stevens. Too good for this place, that's for sure. I'm just glad you've seen sense at last. Who knows, you could even come and work for the D.U.B. when you're older,' he added smugly.

Bop nodded, hiding his face behind the handkerchief as he tried not to laugh.

'Now, if you'll just let me have the keys, there'll be no need for bulldozers and mess,' continued Percival Rugg sharply. 'I can simply lock the school and then send in our men to board it up. At least this way you can all leave with some dignity.'

Bop's shoulders slumped and he bowed his head. 'OK, Mr Rugg. I'll go and get them for you,' he said meekly. He trudged back across the playground and then stopped. He could see his classmates peering through the broken window at him and he gave them a sly smile before turning round to face Percival Rugg again.

'Oh. I almost forgot,' added Bop. 'We want to give you a little something from the school as well. A present, just to show you that there's no hard feelings,' he smiled. Percival Rugg watched him from the safety of his cab. He still didn't trust

105

these kids. They might be hatching something.

'But what harm can come to you if you just stay put, Percy?' he muttered, mulling it over in his mind. 'All you've got to do is take the keys and stupid gift through the window.'

Percival Rugg licked his lips enticingly and watched Bop Stevens disappear back into the kitchen again. He could hardly believe it. All he needed was those keys, and for the staff and pupils to leave quietly and sensibly, and then his problems would be well and truly over.

Percival Rugg gripped the steering wheel and waited impatiently for Bop's return, making a mental note …

What are the two best sounds in the world? The answer, of course, is simple. It is the melodic jingle jangle of keys in locks and that oh-so-perfect pitch of a door slamming, shut – for ever.

Chapter 10
Special Delivery

'Wot a performance!' said Stamford, patting Bop heartily on the back. 'I really fort those tears was for real.'

Bop threw the tea towel down on the work surface where a package was hastily being wrapped. 'Let's just hope he takes the present,' he replied, as one by one M*sss* Bicep-Tricep's toads – Lucan, Heathcote, Bobby and Flo – were being carefully placed into a deluxe-sized chocolate box, alongside the caretaker's big bunch of keys.

'This won't take long, guys,' Benjy said kindly to the toads as he made a couple of air holes and then put the lid on the box. He handed the package to Bop. 'Good luck,' he grinned as a croak came from inside.

'Sssh.' Benjy put his face up close to it. 'Don't make a sound, especially you, Bobby,' he

added sternly, referring to M*sss* Bicep-
Tricep's most boisterous pet.

Carefully, as though he were holding a
ticking bomb, Bop carried the box out into the
playground and across to Percival Rugg's
bulldozer.

'Where are the keys?' snapped the
Inspector impatiently. 'I don't want your silly
chocolates. I just want those keys.'

'They're inside, Sir,' replied Bop. 'You see,
the chocolates and the keys are our very
special gift to you.' He shook the box lightly
and it jingled, but luckily, it didn't croak.

Percival Rugg tutted crossly as he eagerly
held out his hands through the window. 'Give
me the box. Quickly, boy!' he snapped selfishly.
His fingers grabbed the package greedily and
he pulled it into his cab.

Bop watched as Percival Rugg placed the
box on his lap and hurriedly untied the ribbon
wrapped around it.

'You didn't honestly think that I'd actually
eat anything that has been near those dinner
ladies, did you?' Percival Rugg said rudely, his
bony fingers fumbling to prise open the lid. 'I
just want those keys!' he hissed. 'I must have
those keys!' he muttered. 'And then the school

will be all mine. Mine! Mine!'

He pulled the lid off triumphantly, his beady eyes shining in anticipation as he checked its contents. However, his expression soon changed to one of horror as the first toad to leap out of the box – was the boisterous Bobby. He landed on top of Percival Rugg's head and was closely followed by the others. Lucan hopped on to the dashboard whilst Heathcote and Flo vaulted on to the seat beside him.

'Ah! Get away, you disgusting creatures,' screeched Percival Rugg, pushing the box off his lap and struggling to open his cab door as they croaked around him. Finally, with Bobby still perched precariously on top of his balding head, he managed to open the door and clamber out.

Percival Rugg rounded angrily on Bop Stevens, his face blazing. 'You foul, despicable child!' he cried, looming over him, as Bop hastily stepped out of his way. He'd never seen the Rugg Rat look this angry. 'You tricked me, again!' He pointed to the top of his head. 'Conned by a box of treacherous toads!'

Bop could hardly contain his laughter as the pupils and teachers began to emerge from their hiding places. Percival Rugg stared in distaste back inside his cab. He could see the bunch of keys lying enticingly within reach on the seat, but the toads had surrounded them now as if they were guarding them. Percival Rugg shuddered. He couldn't possibly touch those horrible, loathsome things. Not even for the D.U.B.

Suddenly, Hogan, who'd decided to climb back up on the roof, shouted down. 'Hey! Something's heading straight towards us. It looks like a helicopter, man.'

Everyone, including Percival Rugg, looked skyward. The sound of advancing propeller blades could now be heard and then it came into view, rising up over the roof of the school like an enormous winged insect and then into the playground. Hogan waved both arms wildly in the air.

'Do you think it's come to save us?' Benjy asked hopefully. 'Look what's written on the side.' His classmates squinted up towards the machine, as it hovered overhead. It was clearly marked, 'North Wales Air-Sea Rescue Unit'.

Percival Rugg glared up at the whirring machine and waved his fist angrily. 'You've no business being here,' he hollered. 'This is a matter for the D.U.B. Get back to the coast where you belong. Haven't you got any sinking ships or sailors in distress to rescue?'

A moment later the door to the helicopter opened and a rope ladder was thrown down.

'There's someone climbing out of it. Look!' cried Hogan, jumping up and down with such excitement he slid down the roof, grabbing hold of a chimney pot just in time to save himself.

Sure enough, a moment later, the stout figure of a woman emerged. Her hair was tinged lilac and she was wearing a sharply-tailored, expensive suit. In one hand she was holding a handbag and in the other, a big fat cigar.

'It's M*sss* Bicep-Tricep!' shouted Bop as the sturdy figure of St. Misbehaviour's' Head Teacher carefully put the bag over one arm,

shoved the cigar in her mouth, and began her descent. Percival Rugg, aghast, watched as Msss Bicep-Tricep swung perilously back and forth like a trapeze artist, the helicopter blades thudding above her. When she reached the bottom rung, she jumped off the ladder and landed nimbly on the roof of the bulldozer. Msss Bicep-Tricep shielded her eyes and smiled up at the pilot, giving him the thumbs up sign. The pilot waved back and headed swiftly off. Hands on hips, the Head Teacher, beamed back at her pupils and staff from her landing pad.

'Cor, Msss Bicep-Tricep, that was really awesome,' gasped Benjy.

'Great swooping seagulls, Msss B. What an entrance,' said Mr Bateau admiringly.

The Head Teacher stubbed out her cigar on

the roof and then smoothed back her windswept hair. 'I'm afraid my car broke down when I was driving back,' she announced. 'But luckily a couple of my friends from the Air Sea Rescue Unit just happened to be passing overhead, recognized me and gave me a lift all the way home.' She gave Percival Rugg one of her infamous icy looks. 'And it seems that I got here just in time, by the looks of things.'

The staff and pupils stared in awe at their Head Teacher. Fortunately, M*sss* Bicep-Tricep had loads of friends the length and breadth of the country.

Percival Rugg, meanwhile, scowled to himself. Was there no end to this ghastly woman's popularity? What was the attraction? She smoked foul-smelling cigars, kept loathsome toads and gambled like a mad woman for goodness' sake!

'Well, it would appear that *my* machine was bigger than *your* machine, Mr Yugg,' she announced drolly, as two of her pupils stepped forward to help her down.

'You won't get away with this, you know,' snapped Percival Rugg. 'I've unearthed some more information. It's about your dinner ladies and their little culinary capers.'

Philomena and Whitney averted their gaze shamefully. M*sss* Bicep-Tricep, however, merely shrugged and plucked Bobby from the top of the Inspector's head. Then, she indicated towards the tangled mass of gates as a large truck trundled over them and into the playground.

'It looks as if the TV crew's back again,' she remarked. 'They'll probably be very interested when I tell them all about your exploits with a bulldozer, Mr Slugg?' She raised an eyebrow questioningly towards the Chief Inspector. 'Surely you weren't thinking of demolishing an entire school full of poor, innocent children?'

Percival Rugg looked uncomfortable as he loosened his tie. Perhaps he'd acted a little recklessly. The Pinks kid's unfortunate accident was certainly going to take some explaining. He squirmed in his suit as 7R proceeded to tell M*sss* Bicep-Tricep all about Mungo's heroic act.

Simon, the director, had joined them and was listening intently. 'Was this particular boy wearing an over-sized coat and cap, by any chance?' he frowned.

'Yeah, that's right,' nodded Stamford solemnly.

114

'Well, I've just seen him climbing out of a manhole as we drove into the playground,' announced Simon. 'He was being assisted by a man covered in paint.'

'Mr Costello!' everyone shouted in unison and sure enough, heading towards them was a dusty-looking Mungo Pinks and their Art teacher, who seemed particularly stressed.

'Mungo! You weren't flattened!' declared Stamford.

Mungo shook his head and stared gratefully up at his Art teacher. 'Mr Costello's new hiding place is down the manhole that's right beside the gates. He heard what was happening and luckily managed to grab me and pulled me down into it just in time.'

'Normally I don't like being disturbed when I'm planning my next creation,' said the Art teacher. 'But in Mungo's case I made an exception.'

Simon surveyed the surroundings. 'This place is certainly a mess,' he remarked. 'What's been going on? We really need to begin filming again soon. I hope there's some food left to cook with,' he grinned.

Percival Rugg looked on bitterly as M*sss* Bicep-Tricep took the director to one side and proceeded to explain very calmly all about Whitney and Philomena's dodgy past.

'So you'll probably be looking for some other dinner ladies to host your cookery programme now, won't you?' sighed Philomena despondently as Benjy patted her sympathetically on the arm.

Simon shook his head, his face breaking into a broad smile. 'Ex cons? Hosting a cookery programme?' he beamed. 'It's *so* original. We'll simply change the name. How about *Rogues in Overalls* or *Cooking with Cons*. That's got a nice ring to it, wouldn't you agree?'

Percival Rugg's mood darkened. He couldn't believe his ears. 'Are you all stark staring *mad*?' he bellowed.

'No, Mr Rugg, only you,' said Crystal stepping forward. 'You ought to be ashamed of yourself, picking on poor defenceless children like us.'

Percival Rugg stared back at her, quivering with indignation. Poor defenceless children? Who was she trying to kid? This lot were about as helpless as a herd of stampeding rhino with tooth *and* tusk ache!

Crystal stepped closer, sticking her face to within a few centimetres of

Percival Rugg. 'You're nothing but a bully, Mr Rugg,' she glared. 'A mean-faced spoilsport bully and St. Misbehaviour's will never back down to one of those.'

'Yeah, that's right. Bullies make me sick,' nodded Stamford as Beasley, Mungo and Deadly stared at him in amazement.

'We may only be kids, Mr Rugg,' continued Crystal, 'but we have rights too, you know.'

'You go girl!' shouted Kimberly.

'Yeah! Go, Crystal, go!' added Suzette in admiration.

Percival Rugg surveyed Crystal disdainfully. What an insolent girl. She was definitely a mini Bicep-Tricep in the making.

The Head Teacher stepped forward. 'Well, I think Crystal's summed up perfectly how we all feel about you, Mr Bugg,' she remarked coldly.

However, before Percival Rugg could reply, he felt a firm hand on his shoulder. He whirled around and came face to face with his superior – Sir Gerald Blenkinsop-Smythe, the Second.

Sir Gerald stared grimly at him, flanked by two burly men, dressed in white coats. Percival Rugg noticed a large white van parked in the road. The windows were blacked out and it had a flashing blue light on top. He frowned. Beside them also stood a fresh-faced youth who somehow seemed familiar.

'Sir Gerald! What brings you here?' blustered Percival Rugg, trying desperately to make himself look presentable. The act was futile. It looked as if those runaway rhinos had finally caught up with him.

Sir Gerald eyed him soberly. 'We've come to take you on a little vacation, Rugg,' he said calmly.

'Not to Qing Zang by any chance?' asked Percival Rugg hopefully, although deep down he knew exactly where he was really heading.

Sir Gerald looked at him gravely. Percival Rugg's symptoms were even worse than Rodney Archthimble's had been. He'd obviously lost all touch with reality. He shook his head. 'No, we're not going to Qing Zang. But if you just get in the back of the nice van, we'll take you somewhere even better. Somewhere you can have a nice long lie down, for about six months.'

Percival Rugg looked at Sir Gerald, his expression detached and dispassionate. He suddenly felt very exhausted. Trying to demolish a school single-handedly and being startled by a box of toads had taken its toll on him.

'But what about my work?' He gestured lamely across the playground. 'Those despicable children. The idiotic staff. This dreadful building. It must be closed down.'

'Don't worry about St. Saviour's, Rugg,' said Sir Gerald as the two nurses took hold of Percival Rugg and led him gently towards the van. 'It's in safe hands. We've got a new recruit to take over your patch.' Sir Gerald gestured towards the youth. 'I'd like you to meet Darren. Darren Jenkins.'

Percival Rugg stared at the young man standing on the pavement. His shoulders slumped wearily.

'Hiya, Sir!' the boy said brightly. 'Remember me, from the phone and photo shops? I'm working for the D.U.B. now. I got sacked from my last job for persistent lateness. Anyway, the D.U.B. were recruiting down the job centre last week and they took me on. Great, innit?'

Percival Rugg looked at him in distaste and then shook his head despairingly as he climbed into the van, making a muddled mental note …

Percival Rugg took a seat and glowered through the barred windows of the ambulance as the doors were firmly locked. Outside, in the St. Saviour's playground, he could see the pupils and staff milling around, laughing and joking, having f-f-f-having a good time. He gazed up at the Art room window, the classroom that he'd first walked into on his arrival at St. Saviour's, all those weeks ago. A huge canvas was now hanging out of the window, fluttering in the breeze. It was being secured by Mr Costello and Benjy, and sprayed on it in huge multicoloured graffiti lettering it said ...

BYE BYE PERCI-VILE!

Chapter 11

A Change of Luck

Finally, when all the mess was cleared away, the pupils and staff went inside for another meeting with M*sss* Bicep-Tricep in the school hall. Everyone, even Mr Costello, was in an upbeat mood. Chester had decided that his crush on Crystal was finally over. He'd been impressed by her speech but he'd announced that he was dedicating the rest of his life to closing down the D.U.B. Lee, on the other hand, had come to the conclusion that Crystal would make the ideal snooker date. The only trouble was he was now too scared to ask her out.

For the rest of the pupils it was as if a huge weight had been lifted from their shoulders. Darren Jenkins had now been assigned to monitor the school, but everyone knew that Darren was a pushover. He had been sacked from more jobs than Percival Rugg had closed down buildings. His cousin, Warren, had once been a pupil at St. Misbehaviour's and he certainly hadn't taken any pride in his work, either.

'Darren Jenkins couldn't close down a rabbit hutch,' announced M*sss* Bicep-Tricep firmly. 'So we won't have to worry about him.'

The whole school looked relieved. They could do with a break from the D.U.B. for a while. The students of 7R, especially, needed to recharge their batteries.

'Anyway, I've decided that we're going to have a celebration,' M*sss* Bicep-Tricep announced happily.

'Great noisy Norsemen, I love a good old Viking knees-up,' bellowed Mr Bateau from the back of the hall.

M*sss* Bicep-Tricep smiled. 'I know you do, Mr Bateau, and I realize that you missed out on the last St. Saviour's disco,' she added.

Mr Bateau nodded crossly and glared at Hogan, who slunk down on his chair.

'Well, we'll just have to make sure that you aren't locked away for this particular party,' continued M*sss* Bicep-Tricep, kindly. She addressed the rest of the school. 'I thought we could have a combined celebration of our victory and our new school farm.'

Stamford put up his hand. 'Um. You won't be inviting any sheep to this do, will yer M*sss* Bicep-Tricep?' he asked nervously. Stamford still hadn't been cured of his sheep phobia, even though he was back in the city.

M*sss* Bicep-Tricep smiled and shook her head. 'No, Stamford. This party is strictly for humans only. Oh, and Deadly of course,' she added hastily, as the soppy bulldog gazed pleadingly up at her. 'This is my way of saying thank you,' continued the Head Teacher. 'For all of your hard work at St. Saviour's. After all, if it weren't for the determination of certain individuals, St. Saviour's might not be here today.'

She gazed proudly around the hall. 'The school needs pupils like you and naturally, I realize that these past months have been a strain for you all. So on behalf of the old place itself I'd like to say a great big thank you. Mr Costello has also come up with another wonderful idea,' added M*sss* Bicep-Tricep. 'He has suggested that the bulldozer stays where it is, as a stark reminder of what might have been. He thinks it's now become a work of art, a symbol of freedom. Although,' she added, not sounding too convinced, 'he has suggested that we paint it a rather morbid shade of brown.'

Chester put up his hand. 'Mr Costello's idea is great, but maybe we could paint the school's motto on the side of it instead? "Freedom Means Fun,"' he suggested.

Everyone, including M*sss* Bicep-Tricep, erupted into cheers and applause. Mr Costello promptly burst into tears and dashed off to hide. Any kind of praise for his artwork had this effect on him.

'Too right it's been strenuous,' mumbled Bop to Benjy as the applause died down. 'I feel as if I've aged ten years. I've spent so much time trying to outwit the Rugg Rat, I haven't even had time to think up any more money-making ideas. I'm skint, Benjy.'

'Join the club,' said Benjy, looking at him sympathetically. He reached into the pocket of his jeans and pulled out a few coins. 'I've still got this though. Twenty-eight whole pence,' he whispered.

Bop frowned. 'Remember the day you split your takings from that lemonade you made with me, the same day we realized that the Rugg Rat had been snooping around?'

Bop smiled. 'Yeah. I remember. Bop's Pop, I called it. Cor, it seems like ages ago now.'

Benjy nodded. 'I know. Anyway, I decided that from the moment we found the Rugg Rat's note lying in the playground, I wasn't going to spend this money until he was well and truly gone for good.' Benjy shrugged. 'I dunno. Maybe I'm being silly, but I thought that as long as I had these coins safe in my pocket, St. Mis would somehow be OK. Does that sound stupid?'

Bop smiled at him kindly and shook his head. 'No, it doesn't. I'm glad you kept them, Benj. Who knows, maybe they did help us in some strange way. Perhaps they've got weird, magical powers,' he added, his voice sounding low and spooky. Then both boys burst out laughing as Benjy carefully counted out the coins equally and handed half to Bop. 'Here, these are for you,' he said. 'I know it's not much, but it's my way of saying thanks.'

'Thanks for what?' asked Bop.

'For being such a great friend,' whispered Benjy. Bop smiled and slipped the coins into his pocket. 'Don't spend it all at once,' Benjy chuckled.

'Don't worry, I won't.' Bop grinned

back. In fact, he had no intention of spending this little bit of spare change. He'd already decided to keep it in his pocket, for ever. Just in case.

Outside the school, Darren Jenkins plonked himself down on the mangled gates and opened up his brand new D.U.B. notebook. Licking his pencil like a true professional, he proceeded to write down his very first comment regarding his latest job ...

DAY ONE: Don't actually feel like doing any work this afternoon. Off to meet my mates in the park.

And with that he closed the book, stood up and walked away.

The blacked-out ambulance passed silently through the automatic security gates and swept up the long gravel driveway that led to an imposing building.

The Hermitage Home for Sick and Suffering Inspectors was a grand old manor house that was surrounded by pleasant, well-maintained gardens. It was so peaceful you could have heard a pin drop.

Percival Rugg peered through the bars. He noticed that there were men and women walking aimlessly around the gardens, heads bowed, bundled up in dressing-gowns. Some were being meekly led along by some rather strict looking nurses.

Percival Rugg grunted crossly to himself. 'Look at them. The wimps. Call themselves Inspectors? They ought to be ashamed.' His gaze narrowed as he spotted a familiar figure shuffling around the car park in a pair of tatty slippers. 'Well. If it isn't Rodney Archthimble,' muttered Percival Rugg as the ambulance pulled up outside the entrance. 'I must go over and say hello later. Maybe we can swap notes about the school.' He chuckled to himself as the men unlocked the back doors.

'They'll never break me,' he mumbled. 'I'll just play along with them, act the poor, passive sick Inspector who's lost his marbles, and then when the time is right I'll escape.'

Percival Rugg climbed out. On the long journey to the home he'd had plenty of time to think, to ponder over his actions. Of course his outlandish behaviour had been seen as cause for concern. Maybe trying to mow down the school and its pupils had been a little over the top? And his growing obsession with Qing Zang? That really needed to be kept in check during his stay. The answer was simple. All he had to do was stay away from maps and not watch the Discovery channel. He wasn't going to crumble like the rest of them. What? And end up like Rodney Archthimble, muttering to himself in a car park, wearing a pair of second-hand slippers? No way! All he needed was time to regain his strength, clear his mind and then? Percival Rugg covered his mouth to conceal a smirk.

'Here we are, Percy. Home sweet home for a while,' said the nurse helping him up the steps to the house. Percival Rugg walked obligingly alongside him. He intended to be every inch the model patient, eat up all his cornflakes, take his medicine like a good boy – until the time was right. He stopped when he reached the last step and stared slowly up at the building looming over him. He made a mental note …

Perhaps I can close this place down?

He chuckled to himself as he strode inside. There was life in the old dog yet.